THE PIG-TAIL MURDER

Mike Hilton is on the rebound from a breaking
marriage when he meets and falls for an
attractive girl in a Chelsea pub. Unbeknown
to Mike, this pub had been under police
observation for some time, following the
murder of a strip-tease girl. The progress
of Mike's affair is then violently disrupted by
yet another murder — the pig-tail murder —
and he is appalled to find himself the police's
prime suspect.

By the same author

Another Women's Shoes
My Wife Melissa
Paul Temple and the Harkdale Robbery
Paul Temple and the Kelby Affair

and available in Hodder Paperbacks

The Pig-Tail Murder

Francis Durbridge

HODDER PAPERBACKS

Printed in Great Britain
for Hodder and Stoughton Limited,
St. Paul's House, Warwick Lane, London, E.C.4, by
Cox & Wyman Ltd., London, Reading and Fakenham

ISBN 0 340   15022 X

Chapter One

The zip at the back of Della's black dress had been giving trouble all evening. Now it seemed to have stuck for good. Just for one ghastly moment she thought she was not going to be able to get the garment off at all. Her arms were aching as if they had been bound behind her back and she could sense that Max would be getting restless. In the end she had to squirm energetically so as to twitch the back of the dress to the front where she could see the zip and unlock it. Then she reversed the dress once more and wriggled out of it. In the end the impromptu performance turned out to be quite a success. A little flutter of clapping came from the five rows of seats behind her. She wondered if she might even make this a permanent feature of her act. A stripper who had a real problem about how to take her clothes off might provide a welcome novelty.

She turned to present her breasts to the audience, shaking her shoulders in time to the music so as to make her bosom bounce a bit. From seven feet away the spotlight stared at her, its cyclopean eye showing green, purple, red and blue in turn. The loudspeaker hiccuped as a clumsy join in the tape passed through the rollers, then launched into 'Strangers in the Night'. Della's smile never faltered as she adjusted her little dance to the new beat.

She was almost there now. Just the little black G-string

remained. She turned and shimmied towards the silk draperies which formed a backing to the tiny stage so that the men could have a look at her rear view, wiggled it to and fro a few times and then moved to the chair at the side of the stage. To keep within the Lord Chamberlain's requirements she would have to take up the little strip of mock leopardskin before she shed her G-string. Complete nudity was only permissible if you were absolutely static.

Leila, the thick-thighed coloured girl who would follow her, was already waiting in the wings. The business with the zip had put Della behind schedule. It was vital not to run behind time, otherwise the whole intricate system would be put out of joint. She cut down the business with the leopardskin, posed with one knee demurely advanced in the centre of the stage and let the strip of material drop. That was Max's cue to bring the curtain down.

"You'll have to do something about that zip, ducks," Max hissed at her as she stepped down into the tiny changing room.

She nodded, glancing at the clock. She had a little less than five minutes to be at the 'Paris-Plaisir'. It was not a moment when she could afford to let her concentration wander. Leila was on stage, gazing aloofly down at the five rows of white moon-faces. For the moment there were two sets of street clothes in the cubicle. The unforgivable sin was to get another girl's clothes mixed up with your own. She quickly folded her dress and leopardskin and packed them with her high-heeled shoes in the carrier bag, pulled on a pair of stretch trousers and a pullover, stuck her feet into sneakers and was ready for the street.

Della had been on the go now for eight hours and there were still three to come. She had calculated that in the course of her day's work she covered eight miles, scurrying round her circuit of Soho clubs. They paid her twenty quid a week and she reckoned she earned every penny of it. At this time of night there were always half a dozen strippers to be seen on the move, all identifiable by their stage make-up and the little carrier bags in which they transported their gear—filmy shawls, clingy plastic, ostrich feathers and mock leopardskin. They were hardened to running the gauntlet of male whistles and stares. The danger of assault was nil. Apart from the numerous police there were scores of anonymous denizens of Soho who would move in with knife or razor to the aid of any stripper trouble.

The 'Paris-Plaisir' was fairly plush—for a strip club. There was a side entrance so you didn't have to push in and out through the customers and submit to their clumsy attempts to make you squeeze against them. The changing room provided accommodation for several girls at a time and with your own cubicle you didn't risk getting your gear mixed up. In addition the auditorium was longer and the taped music of much better quality, so you didn't have the spotlight staring into your face or those tiresome breaks in the music.

She was just about ready when Doris finished her act. Doris was a sweet girl but she had the figure of a plum pudding. It was a mystery to Della how she made a living as a stripper. Max had explained it to her once. There were a lot of men who were relieved when Doris came on. They felt that, whereas the glamorous women with the shapely figures would never look at them twice, Doris might be within their reach. She was homely.

"Please, God, don't let my zip stick again," Della prayed as she stepped onto the stage.

She could see more of what was happening in the auditorium of the 'Paris-Plaisir' than in most of the other clubs. The closest seats were only a yard away from her feet. The faces of their occupants were fixed on her body with intent

7

and serious concentration. At the back of the room, behind the second-hand cinema seats, stood a group of hazy figures. Among them was what all strippers hate most, a woman spectator.

Just before she turned to let them watch her undo the zip, she saw a man move forward from the group at the back and make for the door that led through to the ladies' dressing room. A moment later she heard it open and close. That was unusual in itself. Tino, the 'Paris-Plaisir's' manager, generally moved in pretty fast to stop anyone who tried that one.

Her prayer was answered and this time the zip ran smoothly. She made a special effort with the leopardskin and was rewarded with a nice lot of applause. She was still smiling when she entered the little cubicle.

The smile froze abruptly. The man who had come through the ladies' room seemed to have taken over the cubicle as his permanent home. He had tilted the chair back against the wall, and parked his feet on the edge of the dressing table. His hat had been dumped on top of her make-up case and he was calmly watching her in the mirror. His age was around thirty but his features were rugged and his eyes wise beyond their years. His smile appeared friendly enough but Della's heart began to pound.

"What are you doing here? Why can't you leave me alone?"

"We never finished our little chat, Della. You ran out on me. Don't you remember?"

"Well, I can't talk to you now. I'm supposed to be at the 'Keyhole' in four minutes. Now will you please move out of my chair and let me sit down?"

"It won't take you a minute to tell me what I want to know."

He had removed his feet from the table and turned to face

8

her directly. Della had run off the stage in the nude, grasping her discarded garments against her chest. The trousers and pullover which she wanted to put on were draped over the back of the chair he was sitting in.

"Look—I've told you everything I know. There's nothing more to say . . . Now, will you please leave me in peace. I've got work to do."

She started to pull the trousers from behind him. He stood up and seized her by the arms.

"Della, you've got to tell me. I must know who this man is."

"Listen—I haven't the faintest who he is." She was struggling to free herself, but his grip on her was relentless. "I don't know anything about him."

"I don't believe you. If that's true why are you so scared every time I try and talk to you?"

She stopped struggling and stood looking up at him with worried hesitation. The door from the street opened and closed. The next girl had arrived to get ready for her show.

"I'll see you later," she murmured quickly. "My last show ends at one o'clock. I'll meet you at the Mini-Bar. We can talk there."

He released her. She immediately grabbed her trousers and began to wriggle into them.

"Last time you said that you didn't turn up."

"Yes, I know, but—I'll come tonight. I promise. You were right when you said I was scared."

He moved out of her way so that she could fold her dress.

"All right. It's a deal. But listen. Instead of going to the Mini-Bar pick up a cab when you've finished and come to my flat. You know where it is."

9

"Yes, Ladbroke Road. What's the number again? Fourteen?"

"Number twelve, second floor. You won't let me down?"

"No. When I say a thing I mean it."

He nodded, picked up his hat and made his way out into the darkened auditorium. No one gave him a glance as he pushed towards the exit; they were all too intent on the stage. At the doorway he patted the shoulder of the man sitting at the table where 'membership' subscriptions were taken.

"Thanks, Tino."

"Any time for you, Fred. 'Night."

Outside in the street a group of Lancashire business lads up in the Metropolis for a conference were nervously eyeing the carefully posed photographs and signs promising 'Twelve Gorgeous Models'. Fred Bellamy resisted the temptation to warn them that they would be sadly disappointed by what they found inside. He turned left and walked slowly down towards Old Compton Street. On the pavement at the corner a young man had collected a small crowd. He had a guitar in his hand, a drum and a cymbal on his back and a mouth organ fixed to a prong within reach of his mouth. A spotty youth in jeans was going round with a collecting bag. He approached Bellamy, who put in a sixpence and then moved on as a constable came up to warn the musician that he was causing an obstruction on the foot-path.

In his more imaginative moments, which were few and far between, Bellamy liked to think of Soho as a jungle where he was the leopard and all the little pimps and con-men were the jackals and baboons. They scuttled off into their lairs when he approached and then emerged to chatter and grimace at his back. He knew all the tracks of this jungle intimately, was familiar with every gambling den, strip joint and cellar club. He knew the names of the prostitutes who lurked just inside the doors of dimly-lit premises cooing invitingly to the men passing by. Dangerous little groups of short, dark men tended to disperse mysteriously at his approach, and the uniformed commissionaires at the smarter eating places nodded re-respectfully to him. Tonight, however, Bellamy was not interested in the small game of this jungle of his. He knew that somewhere in the undergrowth a man-eater was hiding out—a man-eater that had tasted blood already and was thirsty for more.

He walked down Windmill Street, past the old theatre now converted to a gambling saloon, and the cinemas dedicated to nudist films. On the pavement in Shaftesbury Avenue he paused and raised the flame of a match to his cigarette. He had drawn three puffs when a police car slid to a stop in front of him. At the wheel sat a uniformed driver and in the back seat was hunched a bulky figure in plain clothes.

Bellamy flicked his spent match into the roadway, bent down to twist the door handle and jack-knifed into the rear seat. The car slid away from the kerb.

"Good-evening, Sergeant. Did you exercise your undoubted charms on the young lady?"

Chief Superintendent O'Day weighed sixteen stone, most of which was bone and muscle. He had at one time been heavyweight boxing champion of the Metropolitan Police. He was as tough, mentally and physically, as a rawhide knout and as cynical as they come. Yet he was not completely unlikeable and his faintly Irish accent took the sting out of his harshest remarks.

"I exercised them, yes, sir, but I didn't get very far. I'm seeing her again, though."

"When?"

"Tonight."

"Where?"

"At my place." Bellamy noticed the expression on O'Day's face. "Don't worry. She'll turn up this time."

"And you think she'll talk?"

"Yes, I do, sir. She's frightened."

"Well, I hope you're right. None of the other girls will say a word. They're scared to death of the bastard. I wish I could persuade them that they're none of them safe till we can get him inside."

The area round Notting Hill Gate, where Bellamy had his flat, did not settle down until near dawn. Police cars moved continually in and out of the garage beside the station in Ladbroke Road and almost every quarter of an hour there came the clang of a bell as an ambulance rushed to some car collision or punch-up. Even from Ladbroke Road he could hear the steady murmur of traffic on Holland Park Avenue.

He had arrived home at about ten minutes to one. He left the door leading from the street to the front hall unlocked so that Della could walk straight in, and he put a shoe in the door to his flat so that he could hear anyone moving on the stairs. He wasn't expecting her much before half past one, and filled in time by making himself a cup of coffee and writing up a draft of the report on the ring of drug pushers he had pulled in that afternoon.

As a member of the Vice Squad Bellamy was no prude. He could not afford to be. In the world where he moved strippers were a paragon of virtue. He'd known Della for a couple of years. She had given him one or two useful tips that had put him onto small crimes and she had paid more than one social visit to his flat. With her blonde hair, small rose-petal mouth and round innocent eyes she looked a little bit as if she had just run away from the sixth form at some ultra-respectable girls' school. She had a strong sense of humour which was sometimes a danger to her status as a stripper, for she had a tendency suddenly to see the ridiculous side of what she was doing and burst into uncontrollable giggles. Bellamy had grown quite to like her but just lately she had begun to avoid him like the plague. He knew why. She had information that he wanted and she was frightened to talk.

It was almost half past one when he heard a taxi stop at the upper end of the lane to deposit a fare. The door banged and the engine revved as the cab drove away. The patter of her shoes, loose on the heels and slapping against the stones of the pavement, echoed between the houses of the narrow street. He pulled the curtains aside and saw her down below, glancing fearfully over her shoulder as if she were afraid that even here she might be followed. He moved out onto the landing. Leaning over the banisters he could see the front door.

Several seconds passed before the handle was turned and the door was pushed open. Della took two steps into the hall and stopped. Either she was dead tired or in a daze.

Bellamy called softly: "Come on up."

She raised her head to him. Her mouth was open and in her eyes was an expression of utter astonishment.

"Della! What is it? What's the matter?"

Her lower jaw moved up and down. There was something she wanted to say but the word would not come out. She half raised one hand as if begging him to support her. Then her eyeballs rolled up and she pitched forward on her face. There was something awfully final about the slap of her inert body as it hit the linoleum.

Bellamy lunged down the stairs four at a time. Not till he was in the hall and kneeling beside her did he see the handle of the knife sticking out of her back.

At the end of the road there was the slam of a car door and the throaty roar of a fiercely accelerating engine.

Soho is world famous. Visitors to the Metropolis, whether from the provinces or foreign countries, inevitably head for Soho when they want to sample the sexy side of swinging London. Soho is unique. In no other capital in the world do you find some of the best and most fashionable restaurants rubbing shoulders so amicably with brothels and strip joints, or successful men escorting well dressed women so equably through streets populated by pimps, prostitutes and racketeers. It is a democracy of morals.

But for the more subtle, less professionally organised kind of sex you have to move a bit farther out. The club complex has spread its tentacles out along the Finchley Road, down the Bayswater Road and, of course, into Chelsea. Perhaps the most artful and imaginative exploitations of Man's urge to perpetuate his species are to be found within a stone's throw of the King's Road.

The telephone number of Ingrid's flat was not to be found on any of the little cards displayed outside the less reputable newsagents. She never bent her gaze on any man in the street, or so much as turned her head in response to a wolf whistle. There was no standing just inside a lighted doorway for Ingrid, taking a chance on whatever might loom out of the night. Very occasionally she might be found in one of the more luxurious gambling clubs, keeping a weather eye on any lone man who was winning heavily. Usually, however, her 'friends' were arranged by the owner of the furnished flat in which she lived, or rather by his agent. 'Mr King', as he was known to all his girls, kept himself in the background. To try and find out too much about him was not a guarantee of continued health, wealth or beauty.

So while Ingrid sat chain-smoking in a dark corner at the back of the 'El Sombrero' coffee bar she kept her eyes fixed rigidly ahead, avoiding the glances of several young men who kept looking hopefully in her direction. She would have ducked out of this rendezvous if she could, but she had not dared. Her labour permit was due for renewal in a couple of weeks.

It was ten to three before Bellamy walked into the coffee bar and with seeming casualness strolled over to her table. He threw his hat down on the seat and slid in opposite her.

"You're over half an hour late," Ingrid told him. "I was just making up my mind to leave."

"Yes, I know."

"You told me quarter past two—sharp."

Bellamy was pulling out his cigarettes and signalling to the girl who was on duty as waitress.

"That's right."

"Well, I cannot stay long. They are expecting me back at the shop."

"They'll wait." Bellamy glanced over his shoulder at the waitress. "Large black coffee, please."

He settled comfortably in his corner and surveyed Ingrid admiringly. She was a young woman of statuesque proportions, with the profile of a Walkyrie. Knowing that his eyes were on her she thrust her lower lip forward, turning the corners of her mouth down.

"I thought you had forgotten all about me." She spoke with a slow and careful enunciation. "It is a long time."

"Yes," Bellamy answered amicably. "Long time no see."

Ingrid lit a new cigarette from the stub of the one she was just finishing.

"Why did you ask me to meet you here?"

Bellamy waited while the waitress set up a cup of coffee and a glass of water in front of him. He unwrapped the sugar from its paper and dropped two lumps into the cup.

"You heard about Della, of course." He was staring into the black liquid as if waiting for the lumps to rise to the surface again.

"Della?"

"Della Morris. She was murdered. It was in the papers. Big story."

A plume floated towards him as she exhaled.

"I—I don't know about anyone called Della Morris. I never read the papers anyway. They are too depressing."

"My mistake," Bellamy said sarcastically. "I thought she was once a pretty good friend of yours—while you were still stripping."

"No—no, she wasn't. But I might have heard the name, now that I come to think of it . . ."

Bellamy picked up his spoon and began to stir his coffee thoughtfully. Through her smoke screen she studied him anxiously.

"Ingrid."

"Yes?"

Bellamy suddenly looked up at her and smiled.

"I reckon I've been a pretty good friend to you one way and another . . ."

"Yes. Yes, you have . . ."

"I fixed your labour permit, remember?"

"Of course I remember. I was very grateful."

"Was?" Bellamy was still smiling. "I hope you still are, sweetie."

"Yes," Ingrid said carefully. "I am still grateful."

"Then stop trying to pull the wool over my eyes."

Ingrid started as if she had been slapped. Bellamy's smile had abruptly vanished and his voice was like a whiplash.

16

"I don't know what you mean."

"All that about the shop. That job of yours is a front. It always has been. I know what you're up to, sweetie. You're back on the old beat."

"No, Fred. That's not true."

"Oh, yes, you are. Only this time it isn't a beat, it's a phone number. And that plushy flat of yours. Don't tell me your wages as a shop assistant cover that. The rent is paid by whoever you're working for—you and the rest of the girls."

"I don't know what you're talking about."

Bellamy saw that he had thrown her into a panic. He followed his advantage up rapidly.

"You know what I'm talking about all right." He leant across the table, lowering his tone, but keeping her fixed with his eyes. "I'm talking about the murderous bastard who's running this call-girl outfit."

He saw her eyes widen and once again deliberately changed his tactics. He gently took hold of her wrist. Her hand felt cold and he could feel it shaking.

"Ingrid, you've got to tell me who he is. Can't you understand that I'm not trying to run you in? It's your safety I'm worried about."

"I suppose it was Della's safety you were worried about too. Look what happened to her."

"So you do read the papers after all?"

Ingrid's flash of spirit subsided quickly.

"No," she said dully. "I don't know anything. I don't know who this man you talk about is. Honestly, Fred, I don't know . . ."

Bellamy stared at her for a minute half in pity half in exasperation. Then he shrugged and slowly released her wrist.

"All right, sweetie," he said, placing a florin on the table and reaching for his hat. "You don't know anything."

She did not turn her head as he stood up and walked out of the coffee bar. She had to wait for five minutes before the trembling stopped and she felt ready to face the woman at the cash desk.

Chapter Two

The opalescent red Mercedes 250 SE swirled neatly round Sloane Square and took its place in the single line of traffic moving westwards along the King's Road in Chelsea. At the wheel Mike Hilton tried to master his feeling of impatience. It was a lovely sunny summer's day and his whole afternoon had been wrecked. He had planned this afternoon's golf with Brian Rutland a good fortnight ago and the whole thing had been cancelled at the last moment; Brian had phoned him at Wheeler's to say that he had to go out to London Airport to meet an important American customer who had just announced his arrival. If he could get home in decent time there was just a chance that he could pick up Ruth and they could both go out and have a bathe in the Smithsons' new swimming pool. He knew she'd enjoy that. They had not been doing much together lately. It would be a diplomatic move, and might promote slightly better relations between them. Last night's row had been the worst yet.

He started to move his hand towards the horn button to try and chivvy the driver in front, who was trying to turn right and being infuriatingly courteous to all the cars coming the other way. Then he thought better of it. He had already learnt that with a car as obviously expensive as the Mercedes you had to watch your Ps and Qs. All the other road users were instinctively against you and if you put a foot wrong they were down on you like a ton of bricks. He tried not to think of the traffic and to master his bad humour by watching the scene on the sidewalk.

In the middle of the afternoon the pubs were closed but everything else was on the go. There was a boutique specialising in the latest fashions for the younger woman. Girls of all ages from fifteen to forty were swarming round it like bees at the blossoms on a Bougainvillaea. Farther on an art gallery was staging an exhibition of pop art. The exhibits had been cleverly constructed from bits of metal rescued from car breakers' yards and rubbish dumps. One of the Espresso coffee bars had set a line of tables out on the pavement and at first glance the effect of the coloured umbrellas was almost continental. But the customers sitting at the tables could not help looking selfconscious and unnatural with their luke-warm, non-alcoholic drinks. Highly polished copper and brass kettles, warming pans, horse brasses, saucepans, jelly moulds glittered on the front of an antique dealer's shop, and on the advertisement board outside a newsagent's neat little cards advertised everything from a self-contained basement flatlet to a Swedish girl who was seeking a new job.

A businessman clad in the regulation uniform of the City—dark grey suit, white shirt, black shoes, bowler hat and umbrella, seemed as out of place walking along the King's Road as on the highway from Tobruk to Benghazi. Mike followed with his eyes a girl who was progressing along the sidewalk more or less level with his car. She wore a very short but full mini-skirt which flicked from side to side with each step. She was one of those girls who can make a virtue of the necessity of walking, artfully turning the heel inward with each stride, so as to swing her buttocks to and fro with a natural and liquid rhythm. A tactful bleep from behind reminded him that the traffic ahead had moved on.

The automatic transmission of the Mercedes made this creeping game less irksome. Mike's car surged forward a couple of hundred yards and stopped with its nose a foot from the back of a bus. A youth in a Union Jack shirt clattered down the steps and jumped off, almost prostrating a mother with a small child who was trying to persuade the infant to mount. She was a little on the portly side but that did not prevent her from wearing a pair of extremely close fitting scarlet stretch-pants. Over her king-size posterior the stretch was extended to its utmost.

Mike began to think about Ruth again. Ruth was a bit on the broad side but she would insist on trying to wear the sort of fashions that are designed for the match-stick figures of modern model girls. She was intensely sensitive about her appearance and resentful of any suggestion that she might be too old for that kind of thing. Mike had dropped a hint on one or two occasions and it had not gone down at all well. After having her baby Ruth had never recovered her shape.

Finally Mike managed to get past the bus and actually touched thirty during the next hundred yards. Even that speed was enough to have the wind rush past his ears. With the hood lowered he'd been feeling the full heat of the sun. He was forty feet from the zebra crossing when he spotted the girl waiting at the kerb. He took one quick glance in his mirror and then gave his disc brakes a chance. There was just the faintest little squeak of rubber as the low car squatted just three feet short of the crossing. The girl stepped off the kerb.

She was wearing a trouser suit, which had been tailored by a cunning hand. Its slightly manly style merely served to accentuate her very evident femininity. It was in the fashionable violet shade, and flared out at the hips and the ankles. On her head she wore a floppy peaked cap set at an outrageous angle, and in her arms she carried a white Persian kitten, which set off her slightly severe costume more effectively than any piece of jewelry. As she passed in front of Mike's car she turned, looked straight at him and gave him a smile which contained much more than the usual cool 'thank you—for nothing'. Her head and features were up to the standard of her figure. She was wearing a pig-tail of richly auburn hair which she had slung over the front of her left shoulder. Her mouth was full and wide, the eyebrows high and arched. The bone structure of her face was bold and pronounced, giving a strong curving line to her jaw. As for her carriage, it was superb—graceful without being ostentatious, feminine without being sensuous.

Traffic was piling up behind him. He had to move on. As he accelerated gently away he bent his head to watch her in his driving mirror. She was crossing the pavement, extracting something, maybe a key, from her handbag, and going up to the side door of a pub which Mike had visited a few times. It was called 'The Four Poster'.

Near at hand a car horn shrieked. Mike looked ahead to find that a delivery van had charged out of a side turning to squeeze into a gap in the traffic coming towards him. The driver had banked on Mike seeing him and braking. He did brake, but he also had to steer hard to his left. In doing so he caught the handle of a fruit barrow and sent several hundredweight of apples, pears, oranges, melons and pineapples cascading over the King's Road sidewalk.

It was nearly two hours later that a thoroughly bad-tempered Mike turned in at the entrance to 'Tall Trees'. The barrow incident had taken up a maddening amount of time. The owner of the fruit barrow had been remarkably friendly about the whole thing, especially when Mike had offered to pay him the full value of his barrow-load. Long and rather beery con-

22

fidences and reassurances ("I know I can rely on you to do the right thing, guv") had seemed better than legal action, and Mike had swallowed his impatience. What really irked him was that the front nearside wing of the Mercedes was badly dented, and he had not even got the number of that blasted delivery van.

Mike had bought 'Tall Trees' for himself and Ruth to live in when they were married. It had been the most expensive house in a luxury 'development' on the outskirts of Belford. The developer had used a first class architect and made good use of the natural woodlands in which these dozen or so prestige houses had been built. Each one enjoyed complete privacy and gave the illusion of being set in the heart of the country.

At thirty-five Mike was already a rich man. His father, after paying for his education and securing him a place in the family firm of stockbrokers, had died, leaving his only son a cool hundred and fifty thousand. Mike had inherited not only his money but his father's instinct for the market, and after some shrewd investment had increased his private fortune to something nearer a quarter of a million. He had long since dispelled the suspicion with which members of the firm had at first welcomed him. He had proved that he had a good nose for the market and was an expert at handling the clients. What was more, with his brilliant games record—he had played golf for Cambridge—he had innumerable friends in the sporting world and had brought a lot of new business to the firm.

The drive of 'Tall Trees' was curved to give the illusion of length and add to the privacy of the house. It had been surfaced with a tarmac composition the same colour as a hard tennis court. The house always gave him pleasure as it came into view. It was low and rather eccentrically shaped.

The architect had made subtle use of natural Cotswold stone and cedarwood. The fencing close to the house, and the woodwork over the covered way leading from the garage to the house, were painted sparkling white. Backed by the greenery of the woods and with the light of the now lowering sun filtering through the foliage, 'Tall Trees' looked as if it had been there since the woodland first grew.

Mike swung the Mercedes round the broad apron in front of his residence and ran it into the garage. He noted that Ruth's Lotus Elan was still there, so at least he had not missed her. Feeling for his latchkey he walked along the covered way, or 'cloister' to use the architect's pet expression, from the garage to the front door. The hall, when he entered it, was cool and fresh with the scent of flowers.

Mike parked his golf clubs in the stand in the downstairs cloakroom, washed his face and hands in cold water and straightened his hair. Then he felt human enough to face Ruth. He walked through the hall to the flight of three steps that led down into the sitting room.

"Ruth! Are you there, poppet?"

Mike was allowed to call Ruth 'poppet' only in private. The word was strictly forbidden when others were present.

"Ruth, where are you?"

The house felt empty. His voice echoed through the hall and up the stairs. He went to the french windows and took a few steps out into the garden, calling her name. Ruth was not a keen walker. It would be unusual for her to go out without the car.

He went up the stairs two at a time. To the left was the nursery wing, its door now locked. Neither he nor Ruth ever went in there now. They just tried to pretend that what had been Jill's part of the house did not exist. Once, when Ruth was out, Mike had unlocked the door and tiptoed round what had been his daughter's bedroom. But the sight of the gay wallpaper, the cupboard still stocked with her toys and the miniature four-poster bed with its frills had given him such a painful constriction of the chest that he had gone out quickly and never returned.

The bedroom suite consisted of their big airy bedroom, Mike's dressing room and two separate bathrooms.

He walked through the bedroom, where the twin beds were still pushed close together, and into his own dressing room. The letter was propped in front of the mirror, on the chest where he kept his hair brushes, comb, nail file and stud-box. Ruth's handwriting.

It was terribly eloquent, that simple rectangle of pale blue paper bearing his Christian name in his wife's writing. Whatever message it contained seemed to be shrieking at him from inside the expensive and slightly perfumed covering. Gingerly he picked it up and held it in his hands as if he were estimating the physical weight of its contents. To open it required as much effort as diving off the ten-metre board at an Olympic swimming pool.

He stood irresolute for several minutes, gazing out through the window at the garden below.

There was the quixotically shaped lawn which led the eye away into paths that meandered off into the woodland. And there was the oak tree—the oak tree which had been so carefully preserved. The big branch which had supported Jill's swing was bare now. About three months after Jill died Mike had surprised Ruth in tears under the oak and next day, without saying anything, he had climbed the tree and cut down the swing.

As he watched, a jay burst screaming out of the oak and fled noisily into the wood. With an abrupt gesture Mike thrust his forefinger under the flap and tore the envelope open.

'Mike—

I don't like farewells and this is not intended to be a
good-bye letter. It's just to stop you worrying or trying to
find out what has happened to me. Don't try to follow me.
I'll write you in a day or so.

Believe me I am only doing this because I am sure it is the
best way out for both of us.

Look after yourself.

Love,

R.'

He did not really take it in till he had read it three times.
Even then, though he grasped its meaning, he could not bring
himself to believe that this was happening to him.

The letter, he felt instinctively, was something he must pre-
serve carefully, like a piece of Ruth which was all he had left
of her. He folded it, put it back in its envelope and placed it
carefully in his breast pocket alongside his wallet. Then he
pushed open the door that led into the big bedroom where
Ruth kept all her clothes.

The enormous walk-in cupboard which filled one whole side
of the room and housed her wardrobe was open. A suitcase
which had been considered and rejected lay open on the floor.
Her shoes lay in a disorderly pile on the carpet; she had
obviously scooped the whole lot out and sorted through them
hastily to find the ones she wanted. Her dressing table, set
close to the double glazed picture window, seemed to have
been stripped. Usually it was crowded with bottles, jars, sprays
and the myriad implements which a woman needs to handle
the complicated business of making her face up. Now the glass
top was almost bare, except for a scattering of spilt face
powder. Ruth might have decided to travel light but she had
not stinted herself on beauty aids.

The ashtray on the breakfast table was loaded with the filter tips of the cigarettes she used. At least she had been distressed enough about leaving her home to chain-smoke while she packed. He picked the ashtray up and put the palm of his hand under it. The porcelain was still slightly warm.

That faint touch of warmth on the palm of his hand somehow broke the cocoon of unreality in which Mike had been floating. Suddenly he felt that same painful constriction of the chest that he had experienced when he had gone into Jill's room. This time was different, though. He could do something about this. Without thinking he had begun to move fast out of the room. He ran down the stairs two at a time, his brain racing ahead of him. If Ruth's car was still in the garage there was a pretty good chance that she had decided to go by train and used a taxi to get to the station. He knew there was a good train at four forty-three from Belford to Waterloo. Unless British Railways decided to be bang on time for once there was just a chance that he could make it.

In the hall he almost cannoned into a peevish-looking middle aged woman wearing a sober costume and an absolutely safe hat. She might have been dressed for the kirk on a Sunday morn. Even while he was grabbing her by the shoulders to stop her falling over backwards she managed to impregnate her face with disapproval.

"Oh, Mrs Hall, I'm sorry. Listen, did you by any chance see Mrs Hilton before she went out?"

"Before she went out? I thought I saw her car still in the garage just as I came in."

"Oh yes, of course. I forgot. It's your afternoon off."

"Friday is always my afternoon off, Mr Hilton. It was clearly understood when you engaged me —"

"Yes, yes. You're absolutely right. Now, please forgive me

27

but I really must hurry. I want to try and catch that four forty-three train before it leaves."

She let him get as far as the door before she commented.

"Does that mean you'll not be in to dinner this evening?"

"Yes. I mean, no. Well, you'd better get dinner ready anyway."

"Dinner for two, is it?" Her eyes were studying him with beady curiosity.

"Yes," Mike almost shouted at her. "Dinner for two."

Belford railway station was on the main line from the west of England and offered a rapid service to London. That was one reason why property in the area fetched such good prices. The distance from 'Tall Trees' was a little over five miles, mostly within the thirty miles an hour limit. Mike covered the five miles in six minutes, keeping a careful watch for police cars in his driving mirror.

As he drew up in front of the red-brick Victorian edifice the hands of the station clock stood at four thirty-nine. He scanned the doorway anxiously, half expecting to see it disgorge a crowd of travellers which would indicate that the train was already in. But the three taxis were still waiting for fares outside and several people were hanging about with that look of resigned patience which characterises train meeters.

He parked the Mercedes under a 'no parking' sign, and slammed the door after him as he stepped out. A thin line of passengers were waiting on number three platform, where the London train would arrive. He could see them as he ran through the entrance foyer.

"Sorry, sir. You'll have to show a platform ticket." The uniformed official at the barrier was holding a hand out to bar Mike's progress.

Cursing at the delay he went to the automatic machine standing against the wall opposite the ticket office. He had a full pocket of change but not the requisite coppers. He had to stand fuming at the ticket window while a deaf old lady tried to reserve a seat on the Taunton train for the following Friday. It was already train time as he ran across the bridge to platform three.

Half a dozen passengers glanced round with expressions of pity as he bounded down the steps. The train was not even in sight yet. He felt a fool as he hurried along the platform, wishing that he knew at least what coloured clothes she was wearing. There was no sign of her. He was retracing his steps more slowly when he saw a familiar suitcase on the seat just outside the waiting room. He went to the door and pushed it open. The slightly musty, airless smell hit him as he went in. A seedy looking man with a canvas bag at his feet was sitting on the bench opposite, munching at a very stale Cornish pasty. His tired eyes switched up to study Mike.

Mike did not see Ruth till he was right inside the room. She was behind the door, which had partially obscured her when it had opened.

She was scanning a copy of *Harper's Bazaar* and did not look up, even when the door closed quietly on its spring.

"Ruth."

She glanced up and an expression half of pain and half of compassion flitted across her face.

"Mike! How did you know —"

"Your car was in the garage, so I guessed you must be taking the train."

"But I thought you were playing golf —"

"It was cancelled. Brian couldn't make it."

"You found my note?"

"Yes. Listen, Ruth —"

"No, Mike. Please —" She had closed the magazine and was starting to pull on a pair of white gloves. "I wish you hadn't followed me. That's why I left while you weren't there, to avoid having a scene like this."

The man had stopped munching, though his mouth was still full of pasty. He did not want to miss a word of this conversation. Mike sat down on the bench beside Ruth. Somewhere outside a train whistled faintly.

"You didn't honestly think I'd let you simply walk out of my life like that? Surely you realised that I'm not the kind of person just to read your note and leave it at that."

"I thought you might try to be sensible—yes."

"You call this being sensible?"

She turned her face away from him, blinking rapidly to disperse the moisture that was forming in her eyes. Without being able to help it Mike had raised his voice and hardened the tone.

"Mike, I don't want us to have another row. Not here, of all places."

Mike stared straight at the man with the canvas bag, who lowered his eyes and pretended to rummage for something more to eat.

"Listen, Ruth," he said more carefully and softly. "I'm sorry about last night. I know it was my fault. I realise that now. I lost my temper. But you must know that I didn't mean half the things I said."

She turned to look at him and already he could feel the distance between them growing.

"I wonder if you realise just how deeply you wound me when you say things like you did. And it wasn't just last night —"

"I know! That's the point. We've had rows before but we've always made it up."

Ruth shook her head. She had gathered together her magazine and handbag and was preparing to stand up.

"During the past year we've had a succession of rows, each worse than the one before. I can't go on living like that, Mike. I can't stand it any longer."

"The way you say it makes it sound as if it's always my fault. But can you honestly state that every time I am the one to blame?"

"I don't know whose fault it is and quite honestly I don't much care. I only know that I am not prepared to go on like that."

Ruth had stood up. She suddenly looked tired and her body seemed almost to droop. Mike stifled a desire to seize her by the shoulders and shake some sense into her. He stood over her, choking back the torrent of words that clamoured for expression.

"All right." With a great effort he kept his voice calm. "If that is the way you want it —"

"It isn't the way I want it, Mike—but there's no alternative."

The whistle of a train sounded, more close this time. The man picked up his bag and shuffled out of the waiting room. They stood there in awkward silence, while the door slowly closed with its gentle swishing sound.

"Ruth, what's happened to us? Why the hell are we always at each other's throats?"

"I don't know." There was a catch in her voice. She knew she had to cut this scene short or she would be in tears. And she did not want his last memory of her to be a face streaked with tears. "It all began after Jill died. Ever since then it seems as if we . . ."

"Oh, for God's sake!" He swung away in anger. "Don't bring Jill into this. That was all over a year ago. She hasn't anything to do with this."

"Do you believe that? Do you honestly believe that?" He

31

knew that she was looking at him, challenging him to meet her eyes.

"You think I've changed all that much since she—she —"

"I think perhaps we've both changed, Mike." She turned away from him and put a hand on the door. "Now, leave me alone . . . Please leave me alone . . ."

Outside, the rumble of the approaching train suddenly became a roar as it burst into the station. The ground under their feet shook.

Mike said: "What are you going to do?"

"I'm going over to stay with the Harrisons in Paris for a little while."

"And then what?"

"I've been thinking about going back to my old job with Air France. If they still want me, that is."

"Been thinking? You've been planning this for some time then?"

"No, Mike, I haven't," she said with strained patience. "But I don't do things on impulse, you should know that by now."

"Yes, I suppose I should."

The train had screeched to a halt. From the platform came the sound of doors opening and slamming and the shouts of the porters. With the train in the station all noises were magnified as if inside a building. Ruth hung her handbag over her arm and tucked the magazine under her elbow. She pulled the door open. Mike had turned his back and was staring out through the window at the empty platform on the other side.

"Good-bye, Mike."

He did not answer and would not look round. She stared at his back for a few seconds then abruptly turned and went out. He heard the door slowly close behind her, muting the sounds from the platform. A few more doors banged, a warning shout was given and then the low rumble and regular clank of the moving train became audible. The beat of the iron wheels over the gaps between the rails increased in tempo until a sudden hush and increase in light indicated that it had gone.

Mike turned round. Something white lying just inside the door caught his eye. It was one of Ruth's gloves. He went and picked it gently up. He held it in his hands for a moment then raised it to his nostrils. It still bore a faint fragrance. Guerlain's Minuit. Ruth's perfume. He had given it to her himself that last time when they had stayed in Paris, not long before Jill was born.

Chapter Three

For once Mike was ready to face Monday morning. It had been the longest week-end of his life. He had gone up to the West End on Saturday night and got himself well and truly plastered. Sunday morning had been spent nursing a thick head and in the afternoon he had played the most paralytic round of golf for years. He was actually looking forward to escaping from the empty house and sitting down to work at his office desk.

Before leaving for the City he rang up his garage and arranged to drop the Mercedes in to have the dent in his front wing straightened out. Chatsworth Motors, who had supplied him with the Mercedes and several previous cars, occupied modern premises on the old A4, just a quarter of a mile from the M4 and within easy reach of Belford. Colin Chatsworth had been a successful racing driver who had graduated through sports car and formula two events to the really big time of formula one. A few years earlier his name had been a household word, so when he had retired from racing it was a certainty that he could make a profitable business out of running his own garage.

A quarter of an hour after emerging from 'Tall Trees' Mike was parking his car on the forecourt of Chatsworth Motors. Behind the folding glass doors of the showrooms about a score of glamorous motor cars were lined up invitingly.

Chatsworth specialised in continental machinery and was agent for Mercedes, Alfa Romeo, Volvo, Lamborghini and Toyota. The only British make he condescended to handle was the Lotus, though he usually had a few choice second-hand specimens of other makes. In the window this Monday morning was a Ferrari, an Aston-Martin and an R type Bentley with a special drophead body.

As Mike swung his legs out of the car he saw a familiar figure standing beside the row of petrol pumps. On the principle that it is always a sound policy to keep in with the police he strolled over to say hello. Inspector Craddock was a friendly and likeable man in his late fifties. He took a keen interest in the local affairs of Belford and could always be relied upon to give a helping hand to any project for raising money in aid of children's organisations.

"Good-morning, Mr Hilton." His smile was amicable, but something about his manner made Mike wonder if he knew more than he pretended about what had been happening at 'Tall Trees'.

"Morning, Inspector. How's crime?"

"Can't grumble. There's no shortage, I can assure you. Had a spot of bother with that luxurious car, I see."

"Oh, that," Mike spoke casually. The dented wing had been on the side away from the inspector and he had hoped it had not been noticed. "Some damn fool van driver cut in front of me and in my effort to avoid him I collected a fruit barrow. However, we settled it amicably out of court."

"That's always the best way." The inspector smiled and nodded to the attendant as he collected his change. "It's a good idea to report these little things to the police all the same. Protects you as well as everybody else."

"Yes, I suppose I should have done that." Mike wondered

if the inspector had had a report of the incident already. He could not exactly explain that the whole thing had been put clean out of his head by Ruth's idiotic behaviour.

"We've got the orphanage party next week, sir." The inspector seemed ready to drop the subject of Mike's encounter with the barrow. "Can we count on you to do your little turn again this year?"

"Oh, I don't know," Mike answered in an off-hand tone. "They've seen that old trick of mine too many times by now. But you can put me down for a fiver. That'll pay for the ice lollies."

"I'll hold you to that," the inspector said with a laugh as he climbed into his black Ford Zephyr.

"Is Mr Chatsworth around?" Mike asked the attendant, who was wiping his hands on a lump of cotton waste. The man nodded towards the farther end of the forecourt, where an Austin Healey was parked. Mike recognised Colin Chatsworth's back as he stood talking to a tall man in a check suit. They were both looking down at the Austin Healey.

Chatsworth glanced round as Mike walked over to him. He was a smallish man with chubby cheeks and bright blue eyes. He had the rather stooped shoulders of the racing driver and the same peculiarly bouncy kind of walk.

"Hello, Mike," he said, his face crinkling into a mischievous grin. "What's this I hear about you pranging the Merc? You've only had her for a month."

Mike realised that he was going to have to endure a good deal of leg-pulling over this little accident.

"Well, we haven't all qualified in formula one, you know. And don't I seem to remember a little spot of bother at Monaco a few years ago?"

Chatworth grinned wryly as Mike reminded him of the

four-car pile up in which he had been involved during the Monte Carlo Grand Prix.

"*Touché*. Let's have a look at the damage. Do you know Barry Freeman? Barry runs a second-hand car business and sometimes when I get something really good in I allow him first refusal."

Freeman stretched out his hand to shake Mike's. It was unusual for Mike to have to look upward at people he was introduced to but this man topped him by a couple of inches. He was dark and had tight curly hair which grew thickly down to the line of his jacket collar. His side whiskers extended to the level of his ear lobes. He wore horn-rimmed glasses with broad side pieces, and had a long, slightly hooked nose.

"What Colin really means," he said, "is that he unloads on me the clapped-out jobs which he takes in part exchange and daren't offer to his own customers."

"Doesn't look too bad," Chatsworth said, putting his head on one side to examine the dented wing on Mike's car. He had ignored Freeman's sally and Mike guessed that underneath the surface *bonhomie* the two men were very wary of each other. "We can deal with that in our own body-repair shop."

"How long will it take?"

"A couple of days, I should think. Can you drop back, say on Wednesday evening?"

"O.K. Any chance of you lending me something to get around in meantime? I could use Ruth's car but she's gone to stay with friends and taken the key of the Lotus with her. The damn thing's locked so I can't get into it. And we've got this dinner tomorrow night, haven't we?"

Chatsworth stroked his chin and stared vaguely round his property:

"Let's see. What have we got that you could use? Is a Morris Thousand beneath your dignity? I've just taken it off a customer in part exchange and it's taxed and insured."

"Yes, that'll do fine. Anything to get around in. What time are we meant to turn up for this dinner, by the way?"

"Seven fifteen for seven forty-five. It's at the Dorchester this year. I don't like getting there too early. Shall we meet first and have a drink together? There won't be much doing at the dinner."

"Good idea. I'll meet you inside the front entrance at seven thirty."

"Fine." Chatsworth cupped his hand to his mouth and hailed his forecourt attendant. "Tom! Take Mr Hilton round to the back entrance and give him the keys of that Morris Thousand. He's borrowing it for a day or two."

"Thanks a lot, Colin. See you tomorrow."

"You're welcome."

Chatsworth stood contemplating Mike's departing back thoughtfully. Freeman moved up beside him.

"Seems a nice chap. He must be pretty well heeled if he runs a Lotus as well as a Mercedes."

"Oh, Mike's not short of cash. His old man left him something like a hundred thousand."

Freeman whistled. "Some blighters get all the luck. Does he work?"

"He's on the stock exchange. Does pretty well at it, from all I hear. Still, it all goes to show that cash isn't everything."

"How do you mean?"

"His wife's just walked out on him. Flitted off to Paris. She was rather a nice girl, too."

The two men were walking back towards the Austin Healey as Mike's back disappeared round the corner of the building.

"Well, how much are you offering me for this jalopy?"
Freeman's face twisted again in his slightly wry smile.
"About half what you're asking for it, old boy."

On the Tuesday evening, as Mike drove into London to keep
his date at the Dorchester, there seemed to be an unusually
heavy volume of traffic coming in along the M4. As he
approached the Hammersmith Flyover he saw that the double
line of vehicles ahead of him was almost stationary. On an
impulse he flicked on his left-hand trafficator, and steered
over onto the inside lane so that he could filter through to
Hammersmith Broadway. He went almost completely round
the one way circuit and took the road that leads to Putney
Bridge. It was a favourite route of his for dodging a jam in the
Cromwell Road and it brought him through the King's Road
to Sloane Square.

The Morris Thousand's engine was sounding like a bag of
nails. He had had the devil's own job in getting it started at
all when leaving 'Tall Trees'. Now it was proceeding in a
series of fitful jerks, giving the impression that some unseen
hand was trying to pull it backwards. It was already a quarter
past seven. His only hope of being in time was to dump this
heap somewhere, take a taxi and let the AA sort the trouble
out while he was at the dinner. In any case the thought of
rolling up to the Dorchester and asking the porter to park this
battered old vehicle was too much for him.

Progress along the King's Road was dreadful. Even here
the traffic was thick. By the time he had got as far as the spot
where he'd had the encounter with the barrow he'd decided
to abandon the struggle. He spotted a parking space in the
street from which the wild van had emerged, and coaxed the
car into it. He switched the ignition off and left the keys in
the slot. He memorised the name of the street and also the

number of the car, which he had not bothered with before. Then he began to look for somewhere from which to phone.

Almost directly opposite him, when he emerged into the King's Road, were the lights of 'The Four Poster'. He dodged across the street, handing himself off an Austin Cambridge like a rugger player evading a tackle, and pushed through the swing doors of the saloon bar.

'The Four Poster' was a club as much as a public house. It was a favourite meeting place for the *demi-monde* of modern Chelsea and in the lounge bar on any evening you would find the arty set rubbing shoulders and maybe hips with a few of the higher class call-girls. By seven twenty, when Mike entered, the place was already crowded. A strong smell of Gauloise cigarettes and a gust of boozy laughter greeted him as he pushed uncertainly through the ornately patterned cut-glass door. 'The Four Poster' had resisted the Formica and wallpaper revolution and stuck to the mahogany and glass style of the late nineteenth century. Only at the section of the bar which had been set aside for 'snacks at the bar' was there a gleam of chromium. The wall opposite was divided up into a series of small snuggeries not unlike open-ended railway compartments.

Seated at the table in one of these little snuggeries and obscured from Mike's view as he tried to push his way to the bar, sat a slim girl. She wore a long pig-tail of auburn hair which blended almost exactly with her own, and on her knees she balanced a magnificent white Persian kitten. It was solemnly lapping at a pint tankard of bitter. Her response to the shout of laughter which surrounded her was a faint, enigmatic and uncommitted smile. The man standing beside her and blocking her view of the room was a dumpy, friendly little Pole who wore perfectly round rimless glasses. He looked very much like what he was—the owner of a second-hand bookshop.

His name was Louis Dubinsky, and his interest seemed to be focused not so much on the cat as on the reactions of the young man opposite him. Chris Benson was in his early twenties and handsome enough for his unkempt appearance not to obscure his good looks. He wore his hair long, and had grown a drooping, Edwardian-style moustache. His visible clothing consisted of a pyjama coat, a pair of narrow corduroy trousers stained with paint and a long, loose khaki-coloured smock. His lips and moustache still bore traces of brilliant colours. He had never been able to break the habit of sucking his paint brushes and of course his face only got washed twice a week.

"She'll be out on the tiles tonight if you don't watch her, Sel."

Louis Dubinsky led the laughter which greeted Chris's joke. The little party had drinks enough inside them to respond to even the weakest crack. The three girls opposite the owner of the kitten murmured variations of Chris's joke and kept laughing at each other. They were all made up to the nines, ready to go to work at the trill of a telephone bell.

Chris was looking round to see how many other people had appreciated his wit. He spotted the figure in evening dress trying to push his way to the bar and gave Dubinsky a nudge. Dinner jackets, even accompanied by a pleated shirt and green velvet tie and cummerbund, were as rare in 'The Four Poster' as bikinis at the North Pole.

Feeling that many eyes were on him, Mike was anxious to locate a telephone and make his call with the minimum of delay. The landlord himself was serving behind the bar, trying to keep abreast of the flood of orders. Mike reached the counter just as he came down that end to collect a bottle of Stingo from the shelf underneath.

"Excuse me," Mike said in a fairly loud voice. "Do you have a phone I could use?"

Bob West was a swarthy man in his late forties, who had a ready flow of patter and an eye for a good 'investment', specially when no payment of income tax was involved. He raised his eyes only as far as Mike's shirt front.

"All in good time, Mac. I'm serving a customer at the moment."

"It's rather urgent. My car's broken down and I'm already —"

"I've only got five pairs of hands, mate." Bob West turned his back to snap the top off the bottle at a fitting fixed to a shelf behind the bar.

Mike reached for his cigarete case, helped himself to a cigarette and snapped the flame from his lighter. The clock above the bar gave the time as seven twenty-eight but it was almost certainly fast. The landlord had disappeared into the private bar.

"Excuse me," he said to a youth who was leaning both elbows on the counter. "Do you know if there's a public telephone in this place?"

"Couldn't tell you," the youth replied without looking at Mike.

Impatiently Mike turned away from the bar, determined to walk out and find a call box. As he did so he bumped into someone.

"Oh, I'm so —"

He cut the apology off short. Standing very close to him was the girl with the white Persian kitten, the one who had caused him to collect the fruit barrow with the front wing of his Mercedes. She did not say anything, simply gave him a little movement of the head which made it clear that she intended him to follow her. He hesitated, watching her as she expertly carved a way through the crowd, and then began to move after her. Presumably she had heard his request and was leading him to the call box, but for all he knew this was the latest Chelsea style in pick-ups. Still, she did not appear to fall into that category. She was dressed this evening in a brief trapeze style dress which revealed a tapered pair of legs. Most of the men turned to stare at her as she passed, and then switched to Mike with amused interest. Over at the snuggery by the wall Dubinsky was watching the little procession with absorbed attention.

When she reached the wall she glanced round to make sure he was following, then opened a door which had not been readily visible since it fitted in with the mahogany panelling of the saloon bar. She went through the door and for a moment Mike hesitated before following her. He had a suspicion that he was crossing a kind of Rubicon and that something more than a telephone call must be involved in the next step. She gave him an impatient jerk of the head. He threw a quick look at the sea of faces watching him, then followed her into the dark corridor.

She was already ascending a flight of stairs, protected by brass strips on the outer edge of each step. The only lighting came from a twenty-five watt bulb in a converted oil lamp, but the place had a clean smell of paint and polish. On the landing at the top stood a table with a sad and drooping fern and a tray of dirty glasses and cups. She walked past it, still fondling the kitten, and opened the door on the left of the landing.

She switched on the light and went in. It was too late to turn back now so he followed her. She still had not spoken a word.

He found himself in a large room with two high windows. It was obvious at first glance that this was her bed-sitting room. The room had been rented with its furniture, which consisted of rather heavy Victorian pieces. But she had managed to impress her own personality on this unpromising background. Half a dozen ultra modern paintings hung on the walls. They were done in the style which suggests that the artist had got the paint onto the canvas by some system of remote control, or maybe by swinging head downwards from a chandelier with the brush between his teeth. There was a sculpture carved from a square block of stone representing a Mongolian hugging his knees. A hi-fi record player jostled the heavy oak sideboard and the rather seedy carpet was camouflaged by a Spanish rug of brilliant hue. The illumination was provided by a cylindrically-shaped spotlight which bounced light off the biggest and most vivid of the paintings. It represented flames consuming a charred building.

She went to the large divan bed, which was draped with a white fur rug that matched the kitten and was littered with scatter cushions. She placed the kitten on the rug and then curled herself round it. Behind Mike the heavy door swung slowly on its hinges and closed with a gentle click. He stood a couple of yards inside it, wondering what was expected of him now.

She looked up at him with her quizzical smile and nodded towards a table just inside the door. He followed her direction and saw a telephone.

"Oh, er—thanks."

Still studying her with a puzzled expression he moved towards the phone. Next moment there was a clatter under his feet and a triple chorus of yells and hisses. He looked down and saw that he had trodden on a saucer of milk and sent three black cats scattering in panic.

"I'm so sorry. I—I didn't see them."

44

She bent her head forward and kissed the kitten on its forehead. With an effort Mike collected his thoughts and tried to remember what he had come to telephone about. In the dim light he had to stoop forward to see the numbers. He dialled 944 1200.

"Hello. Is that the AA? Would you give me the breakdown service, please?" During the short delay while he was being connected she raised her eyes, found him looking at her and held his gaze for a long moment. "Hello, yes. I'm stranded just at the King's Road end of Charles Street. It's a black Morris Thousand, registration number 879 D B Y. Could you possibly find out what's wrong with it and ring me at the Dorchester Hotel? I'm dining in the Terrace Room . . . Membership number? No, I'm afraid I haven't got my card on me . . ." Mike hesitated for a second. "Well, if that's necessary. It's 'Tall Trees,' Sunbury Avenue, Belford. The name is Hilton. M. F. Hilton . . . Yes, I've left the key in the ignition . . . That's very kind of you."

He hung up, scratching his head. She had not taken any interest in the conversation, not even when he had given his name and address. While he was feeling in his pocket for a sixpenny piece she uncoiled herself and stood up in one graceful movement.

"I'm extremely grateful to you. I expect that'll be the regulation sixpence."

"You can have that one on the house."

They were the first words she had spoken. Her voice was husky and low, her pronunciation very distinct as if she had acquired her accent at an elocution class. She was close enough for him to put a finger out and caress the kitten's neck. The kitten stirred uneasily and jumped to the floor.

"He doesn't seem to like me much," Mike apologised.

"Silly kitten," she replied and smiled into his eyes.

To break the impact of her gaze he fished a shilling from his pocket and placed it on the sideboard with a snap.

"I wish you wouldn't," she said. "That's sixpence too much."

"Well," said Mike, greatly daring. "You can pay me back next time you see me."

Wondering if he had gone too far he moved to the door and opened it. The white cat fled through and disappeared down the stairs.

"He wants more beer. I'd better rescue him before he becomes blind drunk."

He followed her down the stairs. When they were in the hall again she pointed to a door ahead.

"You can get out this way if you don't want to go through the bar again. This is my private entrance."

He remembered seeing her approaching this door, rummaging in her bag for a key. Was this an invitation to return again some time?

He said: "I have to hurry, I'm afraid, I'm supposed to be meeting someone at half past seven at the Dorchester. Thanks again, Miss —"

The kitten had appeared again, rubbing itself against her leg. She stooped to scoop it up.

"Brooks. Selby Brooks."

As he went out into the street he had a nagging sense of guilt. Then he reminded himself that in view of Ruth's behaviour, it was ridiculous to feel like that.

Back in the saloon bar Sel was rejoining her friends.

"Well, darling, that was quick work I must say. I wish I'd thought of it myself."

Ruby Stevenson had spent her working life in the theatre and called everybody 'darling'. She had blossomed past her prime but with her breezy manner and flashy clothes she still retained some of the aura of her music-hall days.

The strapping blonde who was snuggling against Chris Benson's arm was looking at Sel with a faint touch of venom.

"For a quickie that must be a record," she remarked with her strongly Nordic accent. "You cannot have been up there more than five minutes."

"You have a one-track mind, Ingrid!" Dubinsky's tone was reprimanding. "You think that every male you see is interested in Swedish exercises. You know Sel is not that kind of girl."

But Ingrid was not listening. She was watching the quiet man who had gone to the bar and ordered a glass of mild. She dearly wished that Mr Detective Sergeant Bellamy would find some other pub than 'The Four Poster' to do his drinking in.

Chapter Four

That was a tediously slow week for Mike. He was the kind of man for whom feminine companionship is a basic need. Despite the constant bickering between him and Ruth the mere fact of her presence in his everyday life had been a comfort and an assurance. Only now did he realise to what an extent he had counted on knowing that she would be around when he came home from work, or soon after, that his meals and the running of the house would be taken care of. Admittedly their lives had begun to flow along separate channels; she had her friends and he had his. Her interests lay in Belford itself, his centred on the City and the people he met there. But he could not bring himself to believe that she did not feel an equal need for him and each night when he returned home he nourished a vague hope that she would be there, waiting for him.

Mrs Hall, with her tendency towards bitter gossip, was a poor substitute. She demanded not only wages but an attentive and patient ear. Mike had a shrewd suspicion from her manner that she was contemplating departure. But of course he would not learn of this till she had secured a new situation. He began to dine in London and only came home after taking in a show. But he always slept at 'Tall Trees'. He liked to be there when the morning mail came.

There was still no letter from Ruth. In her note she had

promised to write. Perhaps she considered that the conversation at the railway station had relieved her of the need for further explanation.

The one consolation was that on the way into Town on Thursday morning he returned the lamentably maintained Morris Thousand and collected his own car. He had taken a dislike to the Cromwell Road and now made a regular practice of getting into the City via the King's Road and the Embankment. It took a little longer, perhaps because he usually drove rather slowly along the King's Road.

Several times he had considered stopping at 'The Four Poster' for a drink and perhaps collecting the debt of sixpence that Selby Brooks owed him. Somehow that would be rather obvious and he kept putting it off. It was on the Friday evening, as he was motoring home to change his clothes prior to keeping a dinner appointment at the Debenham Country Club, that he finally spotted her. She was walking along the foot-path at the Sloane Square end of the street, heading in the direction of 'The Four Poster'. It was easy to recognise her by the long pig-tail and the white kitten peeping out of the top of her shopping basket. She was wearing the same trouser suit as on the day he had first seen her. He signalled to the car behind and pulled out of the crawling traffic into a space at the kerb a few yards behind her. He gave a brief and discreet bleep on his two-tone horn. She turned, with eyebrows disdainfully raised, saw the Mercedes and broke into a slow smile.

"Hello, there," Mike called.

She walked towards the side of the car.

"It's you! Did the AA manage to mend your car?"

"It wasn't this one that broke down," Mike told her hurriedly. Women were so hopeless about that sort of thing. Still, he could not start explaining now that he had

49

damaged the Mercedes because he had been watching her reflection in his mirror. "Are you going home? Can I give you a lift?"

"That's very kind of you."

He leant over to open the door on the passenger's side. She came in as a woman should; turned sideways to the car, sat down on the seat and then swung both legs in together in a neat movement. He was already trying to take her shopping basket.

"Careful!" she warned him. "Zoe might scratch you. I'll hold it on my knee."

She closed the door rather more energetically than was necessary and smiled round at him.

"Will this be quicker than walking?"

"I very much doubt it," he said, responding to her smile. "Are you in a hurry?"

"Not particularly."

"Good."

Mike glanced in his mirror and rejoined the line of slow-moving vehicles. This time he did not resent the traffic. He was in no hurry to reach 'The Four Poster'.

"I'm glad you came along. This shopping basket is *so* heavy."

"I'm glad too. I've been looking out for you. I come past here every day."

"Have you?"

He knew that her eyes were on his face. He glanced round and met their gaze. It was Sel who broke the contact.

"Look out!" she shouted.

Mike got his eyes back to the road just in time to avoid ramming the back of a post office van.

"I'd better keep my attention on my driving."

Beside him Sel laughed quietly.

The Mercedes, with its hard-top removed and its two good-looking occupants, drew a few interested glances from the pedestrians. Just as it was passing a large second-hand bookshop with the name DUBINSKY painted over the door, two men emerged. One was short with round, rimless glasses and the other was a slightly starved looking young man with a drooping Edwardian moustache. Sel saw them and waved as the car swished past. The younger man stared for a second before recognising her. Then he touched his companion on the arm and pointed.

"Friends of yours?" Mike enquired. He had seen the elder man say something to his companion and then they had both laughed.

"Yes. That's Louis Dubinsky. He owns the bookshop. The boy with him is Chris Benson. You might have noticed one of his pictures in my room."

The drive had been very short. They seemed to be at 'The Four Poster' within seconds.

"Well, here we are," Mike observed as he drew into the kerb once again.

Zoe was gazing up at him intently. He took a chance and put out a hand to tickle the kitten affectionately. It purred and pressed its head hard against his hand.

"She likes you!" Sel exclaimed in astonishment. "That was a nice birthday present, wasn't it, Zoe? Say thank you to the gentleman for the lift."

"Whose birthday is it? Yours or Zoe's?"

"Mine, of course," Sel said, laughing. "Zoe's not old enough to have a birthday yet. Are you, darling?"

"Well—many happy returns."

"Thank you."

She opened the door and swung her legs out. Then, on an after-thought, she paused.

51

"I'm giving a little party in my room this evening. Would you like to come?"

"Well — er —" Mike fumbled for words. An evening in Sel's company was infinitely preferable to the all-male function at the Country Club. He wondered if he'd have the face to break that date at such a late stage. Sel misinterpreted his hesitation.

"Perhaps the Chelsea set is not quite in your line."

"No. It's not that. I — er — I *would* like to come."

"Good. Any time after nine. We'll look forward to seeing you, won't we, Zoe? And thanks again for the lift."

Mike smiled as she closed his door, but he did not drive away till she had reached the entrance at the side of 'The Four Poster' and put her key in the lock.

Sel's party did not get under way till after nine thirty but by ten o'clock it was in full swing. The record player was vibrating to the suggestive voice of Dionne Warwick, the atmosphere was thick with smoke and the cacophony of voices was audible from out in the King's Road. Every inch of floor space was occupied by standing or squatting guests and in some pieces of furniture they were two deep. The bottles which Sel's guests had brought along as a contribution, ranging from beer to brandy, stood higgledy-piggledy on a table just inside the door. Chris Benson, still unshaven and in the same clothes, was arguing with a tough looking woman wearing a collar and tie. A couple of disillusioned young people lay sprawled on the floor, imbibing vodka and Dubonnet and listing the personalities which pained them most, from Picasso to Billy Graham. Ruby Stevenson, her low cut dress displaying a cleavage deep enough to conceal the *Good Food Guide*, was retelling jokes that had died twenty years ago. The two call-girls, Iris and Vida, who secretly envied Sel for her debonair independence, were curled up together on her divan bed. They had glasses of sparkling Burgundy in their hands and were whispering confidences to each other as their eyes darted over the men present. They had kicked off their little golden slippers, which lay in a pile on the floor.

The other end of the divan was occupied by Sel herself. She was wearing a kaftan of shimmery floral material and talking politely to an art shop owner, who, at fifty odd, was the 'Daddy' of the party. She looked up as Louis Dubinsky burrowed his way through the crowd, clasping three glasses of whisky in his two podgy hands.

"Well done, Louis." Sel smiled at him over her drink. "Clever of you to find the ice."

"Here's how. Lovely party, Sel." He peered round the room short-sightedly. "What about our handsome friend with the smart motor car?"

Sel raised one eyebrow at him.

"Don't tell me you haven't invited him."

Sel laughed and looked down into her glass.

"Yes, I invited him."

"Rather odd that he isn't here then. He knows where to come."

Dubinsky was focusing on Sel's face but the light was reflected from his spectacles and she could not see the expression in his eyes.

"He must have changed his mind," she said with a shrug of one shoulder.

"Somebody new arriving now," said the owner of the art shop. "Is this your friend, by any chance?"

Sel looked over towards the door. Mike was standing on the threshold, studying the faces in the room anxiously. He seemed slightly appalled by the spectacle confronting him. He was wearing a very conservative dark suit and a white shirt. Under his arm he clutched a box of chocolates. The two people on the floor had already decided that he personified everything they hated most. Sel uncoiled herself and dumped the kitten in Dubinsky's arms.

"Look after Zoe for me, darling. My hands are going to be full from now on."

Round about midnight the party moved into a different phase. A dozen or so of the guests had gone to a rave party somewhere else so there was a little more space. Just for a few minutes, though, the merriment lost its momentum and it looked as if the party might die on its feet. It was Ruby Stevenson who stepped into the breach. She had taken on board more than was good for her but instead of passing quietly out she had become infused with energy and organising ability. Her old music-hall instincts came back and she set about organising an impromptu variety show. A boy who'd brought his guitar was more than ready to sing a couple of songs to his own accompaniment. Vida and Iris did a rather neat little twinsome dance and Dubinsky was shanghai'd into performing his conjuring trick. Mike lay on the divan with his back to the wall and watched the whole performance with the tolerance that is induced by five brandies.

When Dubinsky sat down to a little round of applause he realised to his horror that Ruby was pointing a rather wobbly finger straight at him.

"Come on! Your turn now."

Mike pointed a finger at himself. "Who? Me?"

"Yes, yes. The handsome gentleman in the smart grey suit."

Mike shook his head. "I'm not any good at that sort of thing."

"Well, you've got to do something." Ruby had rushed over to grab him by the arm and was hauling him to his feet.

"No, leave him in peace, Ruby," Sel protested. She was embarrassed for Mike.

"Everybody's got to do a turn," Ruby announced. "Come on, don't be a sour puss. Just to please dear old Ruby." She turned to the other guests. "Got to do something, hasn't he?"

There was not much response. Everybody sensed Mike's embarrassment and in any case did not want to watch a corny performance. Mike glanced down at Sel, saw that she was biting her lower lip.

"O.K.," he said. "Anyone got a newspaper?"

Someone found an evening paper on the floor under the drinks table and threw it across to him. He nodded at the boy with the guitar. "Let's have some background music."

Mike bowed to Sel, who was looking puzzled at the sudden change to confident showmanship. He folded the newspaper eight times and then to an accompaniment of guitar strumming began to tear it with sharp, incisive movements of his fingers. Shreds of paper fell to the floor until he held a neat, tight packet in his hand. When he unfolded it a dapper little row of dancing girls was revealed.

"That's good," Dubinsky shouted and everybody applauded.

"Do you know any other tricks?" Ruby had cocked a speculative eye on Mike.

"No, that's my limit."

Ruby suddenly changed her mind. "Well, let's have some dancing. Chris! Put a record on."

As the music began Ruby planted herself close in front of Mike. She made no secret of the fact that she had taken a fancy to him.

"Let's see whether your dancing is as good as your conjuring."

The next instant she was pressed against him. Over her shoulder he could see Sel frowning angrily. He was afraid

55

that he and Ruby were going to have to do a solo in front of the whole room, but to his relief a number of other couples stood up to join in and after a short while the floor was crowded. Ruby's eyes were closed in bliss, and she was humming the tune in Mike's ear. Her grip on him became tighter and tighter.

Sel uncoiled herself purposefully from the divan and walked onto the floor. Next time Ruby came swirling past she tapped her on the shoulder.

"Excuse me."

"What?" Ruby said, coming back to earth.

"Ladies' excuse me," Sel said.

"It's nothing of the kind," Ruby began to protest, but Mike had already disengaged himself and was taking Sel's outstretched fingers.

They danced almost without touching; the only link between them was the tips of their fingers. Ruby had gone to the side of the room where Vida and Iris were sitting and was making remarks in a voice deliberately loud so that Mike and Sel could hear.

"This room is getting terribly stuffy," Sel murmured in Mike's ear. "I'd like a breath of fresh air."

"So would I," Mike said.

"I'll just collect Zoe. We mustn't forget her."

Nobody paid much attention to the departure of the hostess. As they reached the bottom of the stairs Chris Benson came through the door from the saloon bar with four beer bottles in his hand. He nearly cannoned into them as he started to charge up the stairs. Then he saw who it was and drew back, bowing ironically and waving them past with the beer bottles. Sel gave him an admonitory look and swept by.

As he closed the street door behind them Mike saw a couple

emerge from a Jaguar E type. They met in the middle of the pavement.

"Hello, kitten!" the man said to Sel. "Party not over, I hope?"

By the light of the street lamp Mike saw that it was Barry Freeman, the second-hand car dealer he had met at Chatsworth's garage. He had obviously been to at least one party, and was well lit up.

Sel did nòt seem particularly pleased to see him.

"No. Mike and I are just popping out for some air."

Freeman tried to focus on Mike with eyes that had gone out of adjustment.

"Good-evening," Mike said. "I think we've met already."

Freeman lurched one step forward, then his face lit up. "Hello, old boy! Didn't recognise you. What a clot! Of course. That's your Merc I parked behind."

"That's right."

"She O.K. now? Old Nigel fixed her up for you?"

"Yes, she's as good as new again."

"I'll bet. Nothing more up Nigel's street than a bit of panel-beating."

He grinned round at the girl accompanying him and gave her a fairly hard pat on the bottom.

"Nigel? Who is this Nigel?"

The girl had been crinkling her brow as she tried to follow the conversation. She spoke very slowly with a pronounced Nordic accent.

"This is Ingrid," Freeman told Mike. "She's a Swede. Aren't you, Swedie-pie?"

He became convulsed with laughter at his own joke. Ingrid surveyed him with an inscrutable expression.

"See you later," Sel said, taking Mike's hand. She obviously wanted to put an end to this conversation.

As they took their seats in the Mercedes they could hear Barry Freeman protesting loudly from the hall just inside the door.

"Don't tell me I've got to climb all those ruddy stairs!"

Down on the Embankment traffic had thinned out and most drivers were forgetting about the thirty limit. Mike and Sel stood leaning over Battersea Bridge, watching a tug pass beneath them, hauling a string of barges loaded with coal. Their gunwales were sunk almost to the water line and a high wave had built up their stump bows. The twin stacks of Battersea Power Station stood out starkly against the orange glow of the sky. Down along the riverside by Cheyne Walk the houseboats stirred quietly at their moorings, chuckling amongst themselves.

"My father and mother were killed by a V-bomb in nineteen forty-five," Sel was saying. "I had a brother but he went to live in Canada and I never heard from him again."

"Do you like living where you are — at the pub, I mean?"

Sel shrugged non-committally. "It's all right. It's free — it doesn't cost me anything. Bob West is my uncle. He's the landlord, you know."

"Oh . . ."

"He's a widower and — well, he's pretty good to me. I help him out sometimes in the bar and he lets me do what I want the rest of the time. But what about you?"

Sel turned round and placed her back against the bridge.

"What about me?"

"Are you married?"

Mike hesitated while the last of the barges slid silently beneath him.

"Yes — I am married."

"You don't sound very definite about it," Sel said with a hint of a laugh in her voice.

"We're—not together at the moment. My wife left me exactly a week ago."

"Oh, I'm sorry." Sel's head had come round and he hoped desperately that the expression in her eyes was not pity. "What happened?"

"Oh, I don't know." Mike threw an old screwed-up theatre ticket down into the water. "Nothing actually *happened*. We've been married for ten years, very happily most of the time. Then—it just blew up."

"There must have been a reason."

Mike shrugged. He did not want to enter into the whole business of himself and Ruth and Jill with this new acquaintance. Sel sensed that he did not wish to pursue the topic.

She said lightly: "Perhaps she didn't understand you."

"Oh, she understood me all too well," Mike's voice was bitter. "I'm a pretty easy guy to understand. Two easy lessons, a spot of homework and you know the lot."

Sel laughed. "I've heard that before."

For a moment they were looking at each other. Sel seemed to be searching his face. He felt embarrassed under her scrutiny.

"It's not too cold for you here?"

She shook her head. "Mike, where do you live? Do you have a place in town?"

"No. We have a house at Belford-on-Thames."

"I know Belford," Sel said excitedly. "Isn't it about five miles from Farndale?"

"That's right."

"A friend of mine lives at Farndale. I go down there quite a lot."

"It's very nice at this time of the year."

"Yes," Sel drew her organza shawl closer round her shoulders and moved away from the parapet. By common consent they began to walk back towards the car. A colder wind from the direction of the sea had begun to blow up the river. "I'm going down there on Tuesday, as a matter of fact." She turned to smile at him invitingly. "I suppose you wouldn't like to run me down in that heavenly car of yours?"

Mike grinned back at her. "I can't think of anything I'd like better. Suppose I pick you up about three o'clock?"

"Three o'clock on Tuesday. That's a date then."

He was holding the car door open for her. Her hand was resting lightly on his forearm and her upturned face was only a foot from his. Her eyes were dark green and one brow was arched quizzically. Her lips were waiting. He did not want to kiss her here. There were cars and people passing. He wanted the first kiss to be perfect, long and unobserved. She stood for a second then brushed lightly against him as she stooped to lift Zoe from her seat.

That night as he drove home Mike was not thinking of Ruth, except to hope that she would not turn up before Tuesday.

Chapter Five

"Turn in at this opening on the left. We're nearly there now."

In obedience to Sel's instructions Mike slowed down and turned into what appeared to be a narrow lane. Immediately he found himself confronted by a narrow track, covered with grass and hemmed in by a hedge that had not been trimmed for years.

He stopped the car.

"I can't possibly drive down that."

"I know," Sel answered calmly. "This is as far as you can get. We have to walk from here."

He had made an excuse to leave the office at lunch-time and at his London club had changed into slacks, a summer shirt and a light jacket. Sel had brought a small suitcase and a carrier bag with some food in it.

Grasping the carrier bag in one hand and her suitcase in the other he followed her along the pathway towards the river. It was impossible not to make a comparison with Ruth's purposeful stride. When a small gust of wind came along it pressed her flimsy skirt against the back of her legs and spelt out in unmistakable terms the neat and economical roundness of her hips.

"Your friend certainly lives off the beaten track."

"It's fun, isn't it?" she said over her shoulder. "There are no houses for miles around."

Through the gaps in the hedge he caught glimpses of farmland, mostly fields sown with ripening wheat. It was very silent. Not even the hum of a tractor broke the stillness. The only sound was the rustle of the breeze in the leaves of a line of poplars near the river.

After perhaps a hundred yards they emerged onto the towpath running along the river bank. At first Mike thought that the Thames had shrunk alarmingly. Then he realised that the opposite bank was in fact an eyot, or island. The main stream flowed past on the other side of it and the strip of water on whose edge they stood was a quiet backwater. The gently flowing current showed that it joined the main stream farther on. It was a deserted and rather lovely stretch of river but there was no sign of any house. A short distance along the bank a boat was moored. It seemed to be a permanency, for a gangway with rails connected it to the shore and a rudimentary garden had been cultivated alongside it.

Sel turned to look at Mike, laughing at his puzzled expression.

"Come on," she said and led the way towards the boat.

As they drew nearer he saw that it was an old sailing barge which had been converted into a houseboat. The mast still rose proudly from the deck, but over the old hatch a kind of porch had been built to provide a covered entry to the living space which had been constructed in the hold, where in days gone by the cargo of grain had been carried.

Sel walked straight to the gangway, put a hand on the rail and once again turned to smile at him. She climbed the steeply sloping plank carefully, placing her feet on the wooden slats which had been nailed across it. Extracting a key from her handbag she opened the door.

"You can come aboard now," she called down to Mike.

"You didn't tell me your friend lived in a houseboat," he said as he joined her.

"You never asked me. Mind these stairs. They're rather lethal."

She led the way down a flight of steep steps, placing her feet sideways. With both hands filled he had to move very cautiously so as not to enter the barge in a flying tackle.

"Well, what do you think of it?"

He put his burden down and looked around. At first the place seemed very gloomy. The barge had been built to ride low in the water and the spacious hold, designed to carry hundreds of tons of grain, would have been beneath the water line. There were no windows or portholes. All the light came from skylights in the roof. But there was plenty of space. Wooden partitions had been built to divide up the hold into several rooms. The central part was the sitting/dining room. At one end was a kitchenette and at the other a bedroom and bathroom. The furniture was a peculiar mixture of the cheap and the tasteful.

"How do you like it?" Sel asked again. She had thrown her handbag down on a low divan and was walking about the room.

"Very nice," he said dubiously. "But it's a little dark, isn't it?"

"You get used to it. At least there's no chance of peeping Toms."

Mike's eye had been caught by an elaborate cocktail cabinet which seemed quite out of place in these surroundings.

"It is rather awful," Sel agreed, guessing his thoughts. "I'm afraid Miriam is partial to that sort of thing."

"This friend of yours. What did you say her name was?"

"Miriam Jones."

"Does she live here?"

"Yes."

"I mean—permanently?"

Sel laughed. "I know what you mean. Yes, she bought it about two years ago." She picked up a pole with a metal fitting at the end and used it to reach up and open one of the skylights. The air in the barge was stale and musty.

"I see. It's very—er—chummy."

"You think it's ghastly, don't you? Would you mind putting my suitcase in there for me? I'll take this stuff into the kitchen."

She picked up the carrier bag and opened a door leading off the main room. He collected her suitcase and took it into the little room at the other end. He found himself in a bedroom, most of which was occupied by a four-foot brass bedstead. To give an illusion of space one complete wall consisted of a plate-glass mirror. The wall-to-wall carpeting was scarlet, the bedspread was of white lace over black nylon, the walls of natural unpainted wood. There was a strong scent of Chanel No. 5.

He put the case on the bed and went to join Sel, who was arranging her stores on the shelves of the compact kitchenette.

"Actually, I think it's very cosy. I admit the cocktail cabinet is a bit out of place."

"Well, I like it anyway." She pulled a stool over till it was under the skylight, then climbed onto it, reaching up to undo the catch.

"Here, I could have done that," Mike protested.

"Well, you can help me down, then."

She put her hands round the back of his neck, and let her weight come forward. He put his arms round her hips and let her body slide slowly to the ground. Suddenly breathless, she remained on tiptoes. She did not remove her hands, nor try to release herself from the grip which was pressing her close to him. Her waist was so incredibly slim, her whole form so lithe and pliable.

All of a sudden she stiffened. "What was that?"

From the direction of the main room had come a dull thump, quite distinct in the complete silence. He let her go and went to the doorway. Walking towards him was a large ginger cat. It must have jumped through the skylight.

"Hello! Who's this? Another friend of yours?"

"That's Ginger. Miriam's cat. You did give us a fright, honey. Have you come to see if we're burgling the barge?"

She stooped down and gathered the cat into her arms.

"Now, don't fret, Ginger. There's nothing to worry about. Everything's going to be all right. Darling, why don't you mix yourself a drink?"

With a start Mike realised that the last remark was addressed to him.

"But what about your friend? Won't she. . .?"

"Oh, didn't I tell you? Miriam's not here . . . she's away . . . she's in hospital, poor dear."

"In hospital?"

"Yes, they rushed her into St Thomas's on Monday morning. She's got to have an operation."

"Oh, I'm sorry about that." Mike had opened the cocktail cabinet and was checking over the bottles inside. "Is it serious?"

"I don't think so. Probably an appendix. Anyway, I've promised to look after this place till she comes out."

"How long will that be?" He had decided on a gin and french and was wondering whether there would be any ice in the fridge.

"I don't know. How long is an appendix? Ten days—a fortnight?"

"I think they throw them out pretty quickly these days."

Sel had made herself comfortable on the divan, leaning back against the heap of cushions piled against the wall. Ginger was parading formally round the premises, his tail very erect.

"Mix me one too while you're at it, Mike."

"What would you like?"

"I'll have a vodka and Dubonnet."

He mixed the drinks and carried them over to the divan. The brief skirt revealed the whole sweep of her long legs. She was looking up at him as she stretched out to take the glass he was holding.

"Thank you, darling. What are you having?"

"I'm on gin and french."

"Well —" she raised her glass. "Skol."

"Cheers."

Every few seconds the barge stirred restlessly as the current swung it to and fro on its moorings. The faint ripple of water along the planks was just audible. Sounds from outside were very remote. He could hear the ramp of a small engine as someone on a scooter went past along the towpath, but it seemed to come from another world.

"Mike."

"Yes."

"You know about property, I expect. What would you pay for a houseboat like this?"

"What would *I* pay?"

"No, I don't mean you in particular," said Sel laughing. "Anyone."

"It's difficult to say. You would have to find a rather eccentric buyer. Fifteen hundred . . . two thousand, perhaps."

"Yes, that's just about what I thought."

"Why? Are you thinking of buying one?"

"I wish I could — but I could never afford it."

She took a sip from her glass and nodded in appreciation. He saw her reach for her handbag and guessed that she was hunting for a cigarette. He quickly got his own case out and gave her one.

"I've never stayed here without Miriam, I don't know what it will be like." She drew smoke deep into her lungs and exhaled slowly. "It could be rather lonely—especially at week-ends."

Her eyelashes flickered up at the last sentence. Mike held the flame of his lighter to his own cigarette.

"It needn't be," he said, and noticed that his hand was trembling very slightly.

A long moment passed. When he finally met her eyes everything had changed. Still holding his gaze she carefully put her drink and cigarette down on a near-by coffee table and put out a hand. He took it and felt himself drawn down onto the divan beside her.

"Your wife must be crazy," she said.

"Why?"

"To walk out on someone like you. She must realise you're irresistibly attractive to women."

"Here's the post, Mr Hilton. There's a registered letter I had to sign for."

"Thanks, Mrs Hall. Just put them down on my dressing table."

Mrs Hall had a knack of implying that she was continually taking on more than was required by her contract of service. Signing for a registered letter on a Saturday morning and bringing it upstairs, she seemed to feel, was a service that required special acknowledgement. She laid the small pile of letters down and directed a sceptical glance at Mike, who was

67

cramming articles of clothing from his compactum into a suit-case. He had had a single bed moved into his dressing room from the guest suite and was sleeping there. Ruth's room, 'my bedroom' as she liked to call it, had been shut up and locked.

"You'll not be in to dinner again, I take it?"

"No. I'm going away for the week-end. I won't be back till Monday morning."

Mrs Hall pursed her lips, nodded without comment and went out. Mike threw the last of his things into the suitcase and managed somehow to persuade it to shut. He picked up the pile of letters from his dressing table and shuffled through them. The registered envelope contained his passport which he had sent in for renewal some weeks earlier. There were two bills, the usual circulars and an envelope with a French stamp. The handwriting was Ruth's.

Ruth had been gone a fortnight now. Mike realised with a shock that for the last three days he had hardly thought about her. The image of Sel filled his mind.

It had become dark before he had left the barge on that Tuesday evening. Though he was already halfway through man's allotted span Sel had made him realise that there was a whole new world to be explored. The difference between her and Ruth was more than physical. True, she was lithe and slim where Ruth was Junoesque. It was her mental attitude to love-making that was so different. She revelled in it with an uninhibited sensual enjoyment. Instead of feeling that he was being granted a favour Mike had the sensation that he was himself the source of her intense pleasure. There was nothing ladylike about her response. She was like a cat, languid and feline at one moment, brittle and fierce the next. It had been an experience akin to sailing through the eye of a storm in a racing yacht.

Holding Ruth's letter in his hand he had none of the sensations which her farewell note had aroused. Without hesitating he slit the envelope and extracted the sheet of paper.

'Dear Mike,

I am with the Hendersons and Marcel has given me my old job back. Would you please send album in top drawer of dressing table.

Ruth.'

It might just as well have been a telegram. He screwed it up and was just going to throw it in the waste paper basket when he remembered that he would need the address. He opened the drawer of his own dressing table and found the key of her bedroom. The room was gloomy, with venetian blinds lowered and the bedding stacked in an unsightly hump on the beds. He crossed quickly to her dressing table and found the photograph album without difficulty. It was an expensive, leather-bound book stamped with Ruth's initials and underneath them the word 'Jill'.

Back in his own room he could not resist the impulse to look through the album. He had never realised that Ruth had been keeping a photographic record of Jill's childhood. There were pictures of Jill in her pram, Jill taking her first steps, Jill playing in the garden of 'Tall Trees'. He closed the book with a snap, knowing full well the effect it would have on him, and threw it onto his bed. Then, unable to resist its pull, he picked it up again and stood quietly looking at the photographs and slowly turning the pages. There was a whole series of the holidays they had spent together as a little family — Scotland, Cornwall, the South of France, winter sports in Switzerland. The last photo of all showed the three of them, standing against the rail of the cross-channel steamer that had brought them back from their last holiday.

He went down to his study, found a piece of brown paper and, feeling that he was packing up his whole past life, wrapped the album up and secured the parcel with Sellotape. He would post it on his way to the houseboat.

"Make it twelve o'clock," Sel had declared. "That'll give me a chance to have the place looking nice and time to cycle into the village for some food. Then we can have a leisurely drink before lunch."

Even though he wasted as much time as he could in Belford, calling at the post office to have the parcel weighed, he still realised that he was going to be early. He idled along the minor roads which took him up-river and to kill time made an unnecessary detour which took him close to a village called Chapel Denning. It was no more than an ancient church, a pub and a few cottages strung out along the edge of a broad common. Mike decided against the narrow lane that led down to the hamlet and took the main road which by-passed it. He was coasting along, his attention more on the thatched roofs half a mile away and the cows grazing on the common, when his reverie was broken by a loud report. He looked round and saw a small star of cracks at the bottom right-hand side of his windscreen. He immediately braked and brought the car to a swift halt. Looking round he tried to see what could possibly have caused the damage.

Standing by the road on the side away from the common was a small boy. He was watching Mike with an expression of anxious guilt on his face.

Mike got out of the car, closed the door crisply and walked purposefully towards the boy. He was feeling very angry. He had just had the damaged wing repaired and now this had to happen.

"Did you throw that stone?"

70

The boy could not have been more than nine years old. He was wearing short grey trousers and a grey pullover. He had riotous curly hair, steel-rimmed spectacles and a gold plate on his upper set of teeth. He was obviously terrified out of his wits.

"Ye—yes, sir. I'm very sorry. I didn't mean to hit your car."

"What did you mean to hit, then?"

In reply the boy pointed over Mike's shoulder. He turned round and saw an ancient oak growing at the side of the common. Lodged in its branches was a scarlet and white kite.

"You must be a jolly bad shot. Your elevation was a bit out, wasn't it?"

"What?"

"Your aim wasn't very good," Mike repeated, still suspicious.

"It hit a branch and bounced down on the road. I didn't mean it, I promise."

The boy's eyes were very wide and his mouth was beginning to quiver.

Mike relented slightly. "You should be more careful. You might easily have caused an accident."

"Yes, sir," the boy said, hanging his head and trying to look deeply repentant. Young though he was he had enough experience of adults to know that the hypothetical tone of Mike's reprimand meant that he was being let off the hook. "Couldn't think how to get it down. The string sort of flew out of my hands and then it sort of I mean crashed into that tree."

"How long have you been trying to get it down?"

"I don't know." The boy shook his head hopelessly. "Hours, I think. My father will be furious. I mean it was a present you see."

Mike looked at the boy and he looked at the kite. The whole thing reminded him of a painful episode in his own boyhood when he had let a new yacht, presented by his godfather, go sailing irrecoverably out into the North Sea. He glanced at his watch. It was still only a quarter to twelve. He began to take his coat off.

"Well, we'd better do something about this, then. You collect some ammunition for me, old man. Fairly substantial sticks would be best. Not for nothing did they call me 'Slinger' when I was at school."

"Slinger?" The boy's anxiety had vanished. He was studying Mike dubiously.

"Yes. I was a dab hand with a sling."

The boy's face suddenly broke into a grin. He loped into the copse that bordered the road in search of ammunition for Mike.

Ten minutes later Mike called a halt to the fusillade of branches and stones which had been sent flying up into the tree and tried to make a fresh appreciation of the situation. The kite was if anything more firmly lodged in the branches and a more positive attack would risk damaging it. It was unthinkable to admit defeat now. The boy was watching him with an expression in which hope battled with anxiety.

"There's only one thing for it. I'll have to go up after it."

"Are you going to climb the tree?" The boy's delight was obvious. Mike felt himself swell in stature.

"It shouldn't be too difficult! Once I can get onto that first branch."

He was glad that he took the trouble to keep himself in good physical condition. He was just able to grasp the lowest branch of the tree and pull himself up till he was sitting astride it. After that it was comparatively easy to reach the branch on which the kite was lodged. He shook it vigorously, but the kite remained obstinately wedged.

Through the foliage he could see the face of the boy staring upwards.

"Don't stand underneath me," he called down. "I shall have to crawl out along this branch."

It was a very hazardous operation, and before he was half along it he realised that he was well on the way to breaking his neck for the sake of a toy that could not have cost more than a few shillings. The idiotic things one does in order to save face. As the branch bent under him he began to wobble violently. It was hard to tell whether he was shaking the tree or the tree shaking him. At last he got his fingers to the kite, worked it loose and saw it flutter to the ground. The boy ran forward delightedly to retrieve it, while Mike began the even more precarious task of crawling backwards up the branch.

When he finally got to the ground the boy had already dismantled the kite and wound the string neatly round the handle.

"That was super. I mean I was sure you were going to fall. I've got to go now. My father said to be not later than twelve."

Mike glanced at his watch. "Good Lord! We've been half an hour getting that thing of yours down."

All at once the fear was back in the boy's eyes. He swung away to run off across the common, then checked himself and turned to face Mike.

"Thank you very much, sir," he said with careful formality.

"That's all right. Only don't do it again."

He stood for a minute watching the boy as he ran across the common, then picked up his coat and went back to his car. He was smiling to himself. His trousers were stained with green moss but the incident had given him a strange sense of satisfaction.

It was nearly half past twelve when he turned into the little parking space at the end of the pathway which led to the houseboat. He sat there, after he had switched the engine off, drumming with his fingers on the steering wheel. After a moment he got out, opened the boot and grasped his suitcase. He stood with it in his hand, hesitating. Then, on an impulse, he replaced it in the boot and slammed the lid. He began to walk down the path towards the river.

The houseboat looked even more isolated and out of place on this slightly misty morning. There had been rain during the past few days and the river had risen. The current was stronger and the ropes that moored the barge were taut under the strain. A lady's bicycle was propped against the post at the bottom of the gangway.

He walked up the gangway and knocked on the door. There was no reply, so he opened it and called down. "Sel!"

His own voice echoed back at him from the hold. He went carefully down the stairs, watching where he put his feet. When he reached the bottom and looked round him he stopped dead. The room was in an indescribable state of confusion. The cocktail cabinet had been overturned, spewing glasses and bottles onto the floor. Cutlery and plates from a table which had been laid for a meal had been scattered over the floor when it had collapsed with a broken leg. Even the bookcase had fallen forward, dumping its contents on the carpet.

With a dreadful premonition clutching icily at his heart Mike went to the half-open door of the bedroom. He looked inside. On the bed lay a human form, completely covered by the lace and nylon bedspread. He put a hand to the material and jerked it back.

The face, distorted and discoloured beyond recognition, might have been Sel's. The flimsy dress certainly was. Tied tightly round her neck was her own pig-tail.

Even as he drew the bedspread up again he heard a high pitched snarling sound above his head. He looked up and saw the ginger cat poised on the edge of the skylight, its fangs bared. He had barely time to throw up his arm to protect his face before it leapt down at him.

Chapter Six

Mike was hungry. To put it more accurately he felt a primitive need to sustain his body with food. After the first sickness and nausea had come a kind of numbness and now this almost irreverent craving to eat.

He was sitting on one of the hatch-covers on the deck of the houseboat. It was already getting on for three o'clock. Four or five police cars were parked out on the road where his own car still stood. Three motor cycles equipped with radio had been pulled onto their stands on the towpath. A Land-Rover which had bulldozed its way down the narrow track was parked at the edge of the pathetic little garden. Already the alertest newspaper reporters had gathered and were hanging about near the gangway, waiting for a statement. The lonely and peaceful stretch of river had become the centre of purposeful activity. The complex police machine for dealing with cases of murder was moving inexorably into action.

Mike's first impulse, after he had steadied himself with a strong shot of whisky from the unbroken bottle on the floor, had been to flee from this whole situation, to walk off the barge, get into his car and drive to the other end of England. No one, as far as he knew, had seen him come to the house-boat. It was unlikely that Sel would tell anyone of their week-end assignation. If there was any follow-up he could say that he had changed his mind—as indeed he had when he left his case in the car. To stay here and face the enquiry, on the other hand, would mean acknowledging the fact that he, a respectable married man, had planned to spend the week-end on a houseboat with a woman he had only met three times. In itself that was not unusual but when the extra little tit-bit that Ruth had just left him came out the papers would have a field day.

In the end it was the stillness that drove him off the barge, the hush of death and the imprint which the brutal killing had left on the atmosphere of the place. Silence seemed to seep from the small bedroom where the murderer had laid Sel.

He stumbled off the barge, astonished to find that the sun had broken through the mist and that a bird was singing gaily in one of the poplars. Sel had spoken about going into the village so there must be a hamlet not far away. He started the car and drove half a mile along the road in a new direction. Just on the outskirts of a scattered group of houses he came upon a telephone kiosk.

He drew up beside it. Natural common sense had overcome his first wild instinct to flee; by doing that he would be fitting into the real killer's plan, casting himself in the role of fugitive.

There was no need to look up the number of the Belford police station. He knew it already. Craddock was interviewing a suspect and he had some difficulty in persuading the sergeant to put him through.

"Can you make it brief, Mr Hilton? I'm just conducting an interrogation."

Mike made it brief. When he had given Craddock the bare details of the situation there was a short silence.

"Which side of the river is this on?"

"The—er—North."

"Thank God for that! It *is* in my area. Now, listen carefully, Mr Hilton. I want you to go back to the houseboat and wait there. What is the number of the call box you're phoning from? . . . Right. Park your car out on the road where we can see it. Leave everything exactly as it is and do not make any statement till I come."

The waiting had been interminable. When Craddock came he was not alone. Two plain-clothes detectives were with him and a professional looking man who, Mike assumed, was the doctor. They were merely the vanguard of a whole army, which went into action with almost silent efficiency. Apart from a few curious stares, Mike found himself virtually ignored, though he was well aware that a uniformed man was keeping an unobtrusive eye on him. After a few swift questions Craddock had thudded down the staircase that led into the bowels of the boat. Mike had been dimly aware of men moving below him, the murmur of voices as the doctor made his examination, the flash of photographers' bulbs, the thump as a piece of furniture was moved, the tread of footsteps echoing in the hold of the barge.

After an age Craddock toiled up the staircase again, looked round till he spotted Mike hunched on the hatch-cover and came over to sit down beside him. He fished out a packet of cigarettes, handed it to Mike. They both lit up.

"Tell me about Miss Brooks, sir. How long have you known her?"

"About a week . . ."

"A week?" Craddock echoed, shooting a quick look at Mike.

"Yes. You see, my car broke down as I was driving into Town one evening and I had to find somewhere to telephone . . . Inspector, what happened in there? I only had a quick look. It was awful. I couldn't bear . . ."

"I agree. Unless you're hardened to it these things can give

78

you quite a shock. That's one thing they can't show on the films or televisions — the full horror of a murdered corpse."

"I know. But was she — was she —?"

"Interfered with?" Craddock said dryly. "No, there was a struggle — a pretty desperate one by the looks of it — but no evidence of sexual assault. She was strangled. The murderer used a length of imitation hair."

"Good God! Who on earth could do a thing like that?"

Watching him out of the corner of his eye Craddock saw Mike's face twist with horror. A Thames Conservancy launch had taken up station at the entry to the waterway and was turning back a motor houseboat loaded with holidaymakers which was trying to come closer and see the fun.

"Go on, sir. You were telling me about Miss Brooks."

Craddock listened without comment while Mike related the essential facts about his first three meetings with Sel.

"Do you know whether she owns this houseboat?"

"No, it belongs to a friend of hers who's having an operation. Miriam Jones, I think Sel said her name was. She's in St Thomas's. Sel — Miss Brooks — was looking after it for her."

"I see. And the previous occasion when you came here was Tuesday last. Is that right?"

"Yes."

Craddock's tone was not hostile. He was here in his official capacity but he was still the friend who's anxious to help an acquaintance who has got into an awkward spot.

"And how long did you stay on that occasion?"

"Oh, an hour or more," Mike answered casually. He had already decided that what had passed between him and Sel on the previous Tuesday had nothing to do with the case. "We had a drink or two and I invited her to lunch with me today. I was supposed to pick her up at twelve."

"And was it twelve when you got here, sir?" Craddock was watching the dialogue between the Thames Conservancy and the holidaymakers. He hardly seemed interested in the answer to his question.

"No. I was late."

"How late?"

"I didn't get here till after half past twelve."

"And what held you up, sir?"

"A boy hit my windscreen with a stone and I stopped to give him a piece of my mind. I finished up by rescuing his kite. It was caught in a tree."

"I see." Craddock's heavy head swung round. He studied Mike's hand, which was spinning the cigarette as if it were a propeller. "And where was this exactly?"

"It was on the common near a little place called Chapel Denning."

"Yes, I know the place. It's not exactly on the way from Belford to here."

Mike looked sharply at the inspector but his face was relaxed and still friendly.

"No. I had a little time to kill and decided to go round that way." What would be the point of trying to explain to the matter-of-fact Craddock that he had been counting the minutes till he could be with Sel again?

"You had time to kill, but in the end you were late."

Craddock pointed the contradiction out with a faint smile.

"Well, I thought it was going to be dead easy—getting the kite down, I mean. In the end it took me over half an hour."

"And you didn't realise how the time was passing," Craddock said comfortingly. "Are you sure it was that long?"

"Yes, quite sure. It was a quarter to twelve when I stopped to speak to the boy and nearly a quarter past when I left him."

"You seem very definite about the time, sir. You actually checked your watch both times?"

Mike threw his cigarette into the river. It was the tenth he had smoked in an hour and the taste had become foul. He had tried to save the inspector's time by cutting his statement down and now it was being made to sound ridiculous. Was he really going to have to explain in detail about the peculiar challenge which the stranded kite had offered, and the strangely pathetic appeal of the boy with the thick glasses and metal tooth-plate?

"Yes, I am definite about the time," he said curtly. "In any case if there's any question about it you can always check with the boy. He asked me the time just before I left him."

"What time do you make it now, sir?" Craddock asked quietly.

Mike glanced at his watch, then realised the point of the question and showed it to the inspector. Craddock nodded.

"I take it you've fixed the time of the murder?"

Craddock hesitated, then decided to answer the question.

"According to the doctor she died between one and two hours before he got here. That checks with the time indicated by a clock which got smashed in the struggle. It had stopped at two minutes after twelve."

Craddock started to struggle to his feet. The doctor had emerged from the hatch, clutching his bag.

"You won't be wanting me any more," the little man said cheerfully. "I'll let you have my official report later this afternoon."

"Thanks, doctor. Sorry we interrupted your lunch."

"You didn't," the doctor said calmly. "I finished it before I came." He was studying Mike closely while he spoke. "You look as if you've had rather a shock. Would you like me to give you something to steady you down?"

"I'm all right," Mike said. "It's nothing that a bite of food won't cure."

"You know best. What about your hand?"

Mike looked down at his hand. The blood from the deep scratch made by Ginger had congealed over the wound.

"It's only a scratch. I'll get a bandage on it presently."

The doctor turned to Craddock. "You'd better see that he gets a meal before too long, otherwise you'll have him passing out on your hands."

"Don't worry," Craddock laughed and patted Mike on the shoulder. "I'll look after him."

But when the doctor had teetered carefully down the gangway he again lowered his broad buttocks onto the hatch-cover.

"While you were with this boy, Mr Hilton—was there anyone else on the common? Did you speak to anyone?"

"No. I didn't see anyone."

"Presumably he was one of the local boys, since he was on his own."

"I don't know," Mike answered edgily. "I imagine so."

"Did he tell you his name?"

"No. I didn't ask him."

Craddock thoughtfully reached into his waistcoat pocket and produced a police notebook.

"Will you give me a description of this boy, please?"

"Look, Inspector," Mike jumped up and stood staring down on the balding top of Craddock's head. "Surely it isn't all that important—about this boy and his kite?"

Craddock looked up at Mike. His brow was furrowed and his expression serious.

"It could be very important, Mr Hilton."

. . . . .

Echoing in Mike's brain when he finally got to bed that night was Craddock's polite but unequivocal request that he should hold himself at the disposal of the police and not undertake any journeys away from the immediate vicinity of Belford.

He lay on his back, staring at the ceiling of his bedroom, knowing that real rest was out of the question. The events of the day kept repeating in his mind, like the 'rushes' of some nightmare film of which he was both the principal actor and the audience. Poised on the edge of wakefulness he seemed to be two different Mikes, one of them the anguished searcher and the other a disembodied pair of eyes watching from some external limbo . . .

It is mid afternoon. The common near Chapel Denning, close to the tree where the kite was lodged. A police car moves slowly into focus. Seated beside the driver is Mike. He is biting his lip, his eyes scanning the common. Beside the tree the car stops. Mike climbs out. He walks round the tree, staring up into its branches as if to assure himself that it is real. He stands for a while, shading his eyes against the sunlight, making a slow search of the common. Suddenly he seems something which focuses his attention. He walks back quickly to the car . . .

On the other side of the common a young woman is wheeling a pram. She is followed by a boy and a girl, playing with a ball. She pauses and turns round. A car has drawn up close behind her; the boy and girl have stopped playing and are staring at the man who has stepped out. He goes up to them and asks them a question. They shake their heads without speaking and glance appealingly at the young woman. Some tenseness in the man's manner seems to frighten them. He goes to the woman and asks her the same question. Again the reply is a shake of the head . . .

A line of thatched cottages, most of them with neat little gardens in front of them. The police driver sits at the wheel of his car, creeping forward slowly to keep pace with Mike, who goes up to the door of each house, knocks and waits patiently till someone comes to answer. The dialogue that ensues varies: sometimes a curt dismissal, sometimes a spate of inquisitive questions, now and then a cluster of faces in the doorway and a lively discussion. Nearly always the final gesture of a slow shaking of heads.

The figure of the boy materialises out of a mist, but it is a flashback in time. He is running away from Mike across the common, the kite in his hand, with the same ungainly lope as at thirteen minutes past twelve mid-day. This time, however, the shadowy figure of Mike is pursuing him. The common stretches interminably into the mist and instead of gaining on the boy Mike is losing ground. In the end the figure vanishes like a will o' the wisp. Mike stops. He has lost all sense of direction and is engulfed in an impenetrable fog . . .

A clearer picture emerges. In a tree-lined playground a group of children are digging in the sand-pit, playing tag or careering to and fro on the multiple swings. A police car drives very slowly past the playground. The man next to the driver puts up a hand to wipe his brow and the strip of white sticking plaster on his hand is visible. He looks very worried. The police driver's expression has changed from patience to scepticism. Mike, the man with the plaster, scans the groups of children carefully, then shakes his head. The car speeds up and passes from view . . .

"The square of the hypotenuse equals the sum of the squares . . ."

A gaunt man in rimless glasses is scribbling with chalk on a blackboard covered with figures. Behind him a class of some thirty boys and girls stir restlessly, yawn or whisper to their neighbours. Abruptly they stiffen and then all stand up. The door of the classroom has opened to admit the headmaster, followed by Mike. The headmaster says a word to the class, who sit down. He nods to the teacher and the lesson continues, a little more briskly than before. Mike stands beside the headmaster running his eye methodically over the rows of now attentive children. He turns to the headmaster, shakes his head. With a word of thanks to the gaunt man, they go out and the door closes . . .

The closing door becomes a picture frame. It encloses a life-size photograph of the boy. It is an animated photograph, for his face breaks into a grin of pleasure. But gradually the picture fades . . .

It gives way to a group photograph. Three rows of boys face the camera. In the middle of the front row sit a grown man and a woman. The photograph is trembling. It is held in the hand of Mike. He is studying each face through a magnifying glass. The watching eyes recede and reveal Mike sitting at a bare table in one of the rooms at Belford police station. The table in front of him is littered with group photographs collected from local schools. A uniformed constable enters the room. He is carrying another batch of photographs and a cup of tea. Under his arm is tucked a copy of the evening paper.

Mike looks up and an inaudible dialogue ensues. In the course of it the constable unfolds the paper and places it in front of Mike. The headline is visible. It reads: POLICE SEEK 'KITE' BOY . . .

There is a sobbing sound and a cloying, terrifying presence. Breathing is difficult for the throat is constricted. The dull thumping might be hollow footsteps on a stair or the pounding of blood in the temples. A door swings back, revealing a bed. The shape on the bed is beautiful, like a sleeping princess. The features of the face under a transparent veil are calm,

*ethereal, smiling in repose. Sel. Then a hand reaches forward,
the veil is drawn down and the face changes—its eyes stare
bloodshot, the tongue protrudes purple, round the neck —*

"Ruth! RUTH!"

Mike woke shouting her name. He reared up on one elbow
trying to focus his eyes in the darkness, searching for the substantial form lying close to him in the night. A finger of
moonlight poked into the room, outlining the edge of his
dressing table. He recovered his bearings, realised that he was
in his dressing room and alone.

He switched the light on, swung his legs out of bed and
reached for his dressing gown. He'd let himself fall asleep.
That was a mistake he would not make again. He pushed his
feet into slippers and padded down the stairs to see if he
could find where Mrs Hall had secreted the coffee.

The police station at Belford was a newish brick building
laid out on modern lines. Craddock's office looked out over the
car park of the adjacent Odeon cinema. The furniture made
few concessions to aesthetic beauty; it consisted of the usual
plain wooden tables, steel filing cabinets, telephones, dictating
machines, reference books.

Chief Superintendent O'Day had arrived from Scotland
Yard at about half past nine. Caged in that small office the
two men gave the impression of two professional fighters, a
heavy and a welterweight, meeting for the weigh-in. In both
cases, as with wrestlers or bodyguards, their clothes seemed
to be a concession to formality.

O'Day was standing at the window, staring unseeingly at
the car park with his hands clasped behind his broad back,
while Craddock completed his questioning of the woman who
sat opposite his desk. She wore the uniform of a district nurse
and was as brittle and touchy as a squirrel at bay.

"I still don't understand why you did not go onto the houseboat —"

"I've explained why. I was on my way to a confinement. And if there is one thing that waits for no man —"

"Why were you cycling along the towpath? Doesn't the county provide you with a car?"

"The county provides me with a car, yes, Inspector. But things can go wrong with cars just as much as with people. They have their sicknesses too —"

"Your car was in the garage. I see. Now surely when you heard this woman cry out —"

"I did not say 'cry out'. You are putting words into my mouth which I never used. I said I heard 'raised voices'. That could have meant a number of things —"

"In this case it meant that a woman was being murdered."

"And will you tell me how I was to know that? My task is medicine, not divination. I can assure you that if I were to allow myself to be diverted from my duties by every —"

"Anyway, you are sure — quite sure — about the time."

"Quite sure. I had just heard the clock on Chapel Denning church strike mid-day. That was the reason I was in a hurry; my appointment with Dr Denson —"

"Quite so. Well, we mustn't detain you. Thank you, Sister." Craddock had risen to his feet. "You have been a great help."

"I'm glad someone thinks so," said Alice Thorpe, grasping her satchel firmly as she turned to leave. The door closed behind her with an efficient click.

"Little fireball," O'Day remarked as he came away from the window. "Still, her testimony is very positive. There's no doubt about the time. We can be sure of that now. It must have happened as near twelve as damn it."

"Yes," Craddock agreed, cramming tobacco into his pipe.

"Which means that as soon as we can locate this boy Hilton can be ruled out."

O'Day shot a shrewd look at Craddock and sat down on the corner of his desk.

"You don't think Hilton is our man, do you, John?"

"I've known Mike Hilton for years. He's a very respectable citizen. Gives generously to local charities. Never mixes with the sort of people involved in the cases you're investigating — strippers, call-girls, that sort of thing."

"He got mixed up with Selby Brooks," O'Day pointed out dryly. "Do you believe that statement of his — that it was just a nice, innocent friendship?"

Craddock puffed several times at his pipe, made sure that it was drawing properly, and threw the match in the waste paper basket.

"You're pretty sure there's a link between these two murders, aren't you?"

"Della Morris used 'The Hotbed'. So did Selby Brooks. That's enough for a start. Do you know Hilton's wife?"

"I've met her."

"I understand she's left him."

"Well — when you say left him —"

"She's taken up her old job with Air France in Paris, John. Don't you call that leaving him?"

Craddock shrugged.

"What was the trouble, John? Had he started playing around?"

"No. No, I'm sure it wasn't anything like that."

O'Day was finding the edge of the desk uncomfortable. He slipped down into Craddock's own chair and picked up the memo on Mike Hilton which had been prepared by the Belford records section.

"Well, what was it then?"

"I don't know. I think perhaps things have been a little—well—difficult for them just recently."

"In what way? To judge by this memo he's not exactly on the bread line."

Craddock hesitated, peering into the bowl of his pipe as if for guidance.

"I don't mean that. This daughter of theirs—the little girl who died of leukemia about a year ago. Hilton took it very hard."

O'Day pursed his lips and stared back at Craddock.

"That could explain —"

He was interrupted by a knock on the door. A uniformed constable put his head into the office.

"What is it, Roberts?"

"We have Mr Hilton waiting outside, sir."

"All right," Craddock said, after O'Day had answered his glance with a nod. "Show him in."

Almost as if he were disassociating himself from the proceedings Craddock went and stood with his back to the window, leaving O'Day in possession of his desk.

When Mike was shown in he reacted with evident surprise to the sight of O'Day occupying Craddock's desk so confidently. Mike's eyes were shadowed and bloodshot, the fingers of his left hand were stained by the interminable cigarettes he had smoked and the plaster on his scratched hand had become dirty and frayed. He glanced towards Craddock.

"Sit down, Mr Hilton." Craddock spoke over his shoulder. "This is Superintendent O'Day from Scotland Yard."

"Scotland Yard?" Mike repeated. He looked at O'Day with puzzled interest. O'Day had not glanced up when he entered. He appeared to be still engrossed in the folder on his desk. "How do you do."

For a few seconds O'Day ignored the greeting. Mike sat

down nervously in the chair facing him across the desk. Suddenly O'Day dropped the folder and stared straight at him.

"Hello, Mr Hilton. How's the hand?"

"The hand? Oh, this. It's all right, thanks."

"Scratched by a cat, is that correct?"

"Er—yes." Mike wondered how seriously he was supposed to take this question. Was it part of an interrogation? Ought he to explain in detail about the ginger cat? But O'Day was already ploughing on.

"Well, take good care of it. A scratch from a cat can be very nasty. You never know what complications may arise. I've just been reading your statement, sir. It makes interesting reading, even if it is a little confusing."

"Confusing?" Mike glanced towards Craddock, but he had turned his back to the room and was intent upon a scrutiny of the half-dozen cars in the park.

"Yes. You told Inspector Craddock that the houseboat belonged to a woman called Miriam Jones."

"That's correct."

"Who gave you that choice piece of information, sir?"

"Why, Sel—Miss Brooks did."

"And you believed her?"

"Of course I believed her!" Mike retorted in amazement.

O'Day picked up the folder.

"The houseboat was bought from Jackson Bros. of Kingston on the third of June last year. The price was sixteen hundred pounds. The purchaser was a Miss Selby Brooks."

It took Mike several seconds to find his voice. "I—I don't believe this —"

Craddock swung round from the window. "It's true, Mr Hilton. Apart from the information from Jackson Bros. we've checked at St Thomas's. They've no patient by the name of Miriam Jones."

"But they must have!" Mike jumped to his feet. He was appealing to Craddock now, ignoring the hostile, monolithic O'Day. "I just don't believe this. Where would Sel get sixteen hundred pounds?"

"According to this statement," O'Day proceeded calmly, "the first time you went to 'The Hotbed' was just over ten days ago."

" 'The Hotbed'?" Mike echoed, puzzled by O'Day's purring brogue.

"The pub, sir. 'The Four Poster.' Our local people call it 'The Hotbed'." O'Day's rugged face relaxed very briefly into a fleeting smile. "Not without a very good reason, I can assure you."

Mike scanned O'Day's face, the corner of his mouth twitching slightly. He glanced at Craddock and thought he saw compassion in his eyes.

"What are you trying to tell me, Superintendent?"

"Something you must already know, Mr Hilton. Selby Brooks was a bad lot. Just how bad —"

"I don't believe this!" Mike interrupted fiercely. "I just don't believe a word of it. You're making it up to try and trick me into —"

"Don't try and bamboozle me, please." O'Day's voice was granite hard. His jaw had come forward and his eyes fixed ruthlessly on Mike, were as bleak as a hunter's. "You know as well as I do that Selby Brooks was a professional blackmailer and that she had got you into a position where she could milk you for as much as she wanted."

"That's a bloody lie!" Mike shouted. His clenched fists were on the table and he was glaring down into O'Day's impassive face. "A bloody lie!"

"Sit down, Mr Hilton," O'Day's voice had become velvety smooth. "I think you and I had better have a little chat."

Suddenly ashamed at his loss of control Mike slowly sat down again in the chair. The superintendent's manner was icily formal.

"Inspector Craddock has explained to you that as police officers investigating a murder we would be asking you to assist us in our enquiries by answering certain questions and that those answers might be taken down in writing and used in evidence."

Mike nodded. The baleful aggressiveness with which he had been regarding O'Day gave place to a wary defensiveness. O'Day must have pressed a bell, for a shorthand writer slipped unobtrusively into the room and ensconced himself at a small table just inside the door.

"What did Miss Brooks tell you about yourself, sir?"

"She said that she lived at 'The Four Poster' with her uncle and that he . . ."

"Her uncle?"

"Yes. The landlord. His name is Bob West."

O'Day smiled. "Go on, sir."

"She said her mother and father had been killed in the blitz towards the end of the war."

"She was lying," O'Day cut in crisply.

Craddock turned from his scrutiny of the car park. "Her father's alive. He has a draper's shop in Bristol. He's a nice quiet little man—until you mention his daughter."

Mike's mouth had opened, but he bit off whatever he was going to say.

"What else did she tell you?" pursued O'Day.

"Nothing."

O'Day sniffed. He picked up the folder and riffled back a few pages.

"The first time you met Brooks was on Tuesday the eleventh. That is correct?"

"Yes."

"Wasn't it rather unusual to make an emergency telephone call from the bedroom of a completely strange woman?"

"I covered that point in my statement. My car had broken down. I had to phone the A A. She offered the use of her phone."

"You do not explain what made you choose 'The Four Poster'. There is a public call box on the street a hundred yards farther on."

"I—er. It was a question of finding somewhere to park."

"You're sure it was the first time you had seen her?"

"Yes." Strictly speaking it was not a true answer. Mike was damned if he was going to tell O'Day about watching Sel cross the road.

"Well, we'll leave it at that for the moment. Now the next time you met was a chance encounter in the King's Road. Was that not rather a remarkable coincidence?"

Mike appealed mutely to Craddock, but the inspector's back was again turned. He was very aware of the shorthand writer behind him.

"I travelled along the King's Road every day. It was only on the Friday that I saw her again."

"I'm surprised you don't use the Cromwell Road. I always do. It's much faster."

"Well, perhaps I was hoping to see Miss Brooks again."

"Perhaps? Do you not know?"

Mike declined to answer. O'Day left the question in the air for a moment.

"So arising out of that meeting you attended a party in her room that same evening."

"Yes," Mike answered tartly. "By another strange coincidence it was her birthday."

"Lucky girl," observed O'Day equably. "Like the Queen."

93

"I don't understand you."

"She must have celebrated her birthday twice a year. Brooks was born on January the third."

"I wish you wouldn't keep referring to her as Brooks. You make it sound as if she had committed some crime."

"Dear me. That would not do at all. *Miss* Brooks. Now, I'm told that you were quite a success at the party."

"I don't see that that has anything to do with it."

"Perhaps it has, perhaps not. You must let me be the judge of that."

"Well, various people had to perform turns—sing or conjure or something."

"So what did you do?"

"My one and only trick. It consists of tearing a folded newspaper in such a way as to produce a row of dancing girls."

"Yes, it's a damned good little act," intervened Craddock. "It's made a good few bob for us at local charity functions."

"Now can we look again at your movements yesterday morning? You state that you left your home, 'Tall Trees', a little before eleven."

"Yes, five or ten to, I think."

"Yes, your cook-housekeeper confirms that. It was your intention to be away till the Monday. Had Broo—had Miss Brooks invited you to spend the week-end on the houseboat?"

Mike hesitated for perhaps two seconds. "Nothing definite was arranged. I intended to pick her up at twelve and after that—well—play it by ear."

"Your wife has been away since, let me see, Friday the seventh?"

The inference of O'Day's irrelevant reference to Ruth's departure was obvious. Once again Mike remained silent, but O'Day had made the point he wanted.

"So you left over an hour for the ten-mile trip to the house-boat."

"There were one or two things I wanted to do in Belford. I had a parcel to post, for instance."

"Yes," O'Day confirmed, "you entered the post office at seven minutes past eleven and filled in a customs declaration. What else did you do in Belford?"

"Do I need to answer all these questions, Inspector?" Mike appealed to Craddock's back. Craddock swung his heavy body round and lumbered over to the desk. His brow was furrowed and he looked unhappy.

"You don't have to, Mr Hilton. You have a perfect right to say nothing unless you have legal advice. But the super-intendent is only anxious to check over your statement with you so that we can establish your whereabouts at the time of the crime. It is in your own interests, sir. So long as you are telling the truth you have nothing to worry about."

"Of course I am telling the truth!"

"Well then, sir —"

"May I smoke?"

"Certainly."

O'Day's eyes remained fixed on the documents in the folder until Mike had a cigarette going. Then he looked up as if there had been no interruption at all.

"Mr Hilton, you were going to tell me about your move-ments after you visited the post office."

"Well, I began to motor in the direction of Farndale. If you must know I was rather looking forward to seeing Miss Brooks again and I did not want to be late. She had asked me not to get there before twelve —"

O'Day's attention was suddenly sharpened.

"She said that, did she? Now why do you suppose she was so anxious for you not to arrive before twelve?"

"She said she wanted to go into the village to buy some things. Presumably she didn't want to have to get up too early in the morning."

"A reasonable assumption. However in the end you did not reach the barge till half past twelve."

"That's fully covered in my statement and I have explained the reason to Inspector Craddock."

"You made a detour through Chapel Denning, where you had an encounter with a boy."

"Correct. And I have a broken windscreen to show for it."

"Yes, you have a broken windscreen. And you stopped to help him with his kite?"

"Correct."

"But you became so absorbed in helping this boy that you forgot you had a rendezvous with an attractive young lady."

"Correct."

"This boy—you have tried to find him again?"

"I've been to every house in Chapel Denning. I've visited the children's playgrounds for miles around, been to the three schools within a radius of ten miles, talked to the people in the village pub. I even went to watch the congregation going into parish communion at nine o'clock this morning."

"No sign of him?"

"None."

"Why do you suppose this boy has not come forward?"

"I don't know."

"Why haven't we heard from either the boy or his parents?"

"I don't know why. They may live farther away . . ."

"Wherever they live they must read the papers, or listen to the radio, or watch television. You know, we've really gone to town on this boy, Mr Hilton. We've really tried to find him for you."

"Yes," Mike shook his head in bewilderment. "I appreciate what you've done. I just don't understand why he hasn't turned up."

"Neither do I, sir." O'Day had opened a drawer in the desk and dropped his hand into it. "Now tell me about your first visit to the houseboat. There were only two visits, weren't there?"

With an effort Mike switched his mind back to that Tuesday afternoon. He nodded in confirmation.

"How long did you stay on that occasion?"

Mike's spirits dropped. Was it all going to have to come out? Was this implacable man going to insist on a move by move account of the hours of delight which he had spent in Sel's arms?

"I suppose an hour or two," he said casually. "I know the time went awfully quickly."

"No doubt. Did you entertain Miss Brooks?"

"Entertain her?" Mike repeated stupidly. He knew that the blood was coming to his face.

"Yes, sir. Fun and games. Party tricks."

"Are you trying to be funny?" Mike demanded. His nervousness had abruptly sparked into anger. "What the hell are you talking about?"

For answer O'Day withdrew his hand from the desk drawer. He was grasping a folded sheet of newspaper. When he unrolled it Mike could see that the centre had been torn unevenly. Even before the superintendent held it up he knew what he would see: the blank space from which had been torn the little row of dancing girls. And the page bore a week-old date, the Friday of Sel's party.

"I'm talking about this, Mr Hilton."

D   97

Mike was staring incredulously at the sheet of newspaper. "Where—did you find that?"

O'Day glanced up at Craddock as if inviting him to take some part in the interrogation. Craddock had moved over to stand at Mike's shoulder.

He said: "We found it on the houseboat."

Chapter Seven

There was silence in the inspector's office after Mike had been shown out. Craddock had taken up his favourite stance at the window, brooding over the car park with his hands clasped behind his broad back. O'Day was scribbling notes on a memo pad and the whisper of his pen as it raced over the paper was the only sound from inside the room. The shorthand typist had gone off to prepare a transcript of the interview.

After perhaps five minutes the superintendent threw down his pen and pushed the chair back.

"Well," said Craddock. "What was your impression of him?"

"Pretty well what I expected. Nervous, cagey, thinking out his answers carefully before committing himself. I'm not satisfied. There are too many things about his statements that don't add up."

"This business about having time to kill yesterday and then turning up half an hour behind time?"

"If he did turn up half an hour late," O'Day pointed out. "We only have his word for that, you know."

"Yes, I know, Tiny." Craddock picked up his pipe which had been deposited in the ashtray and began to dig out the dottle with a squat penknife. "But if Hilton killed Brooks why did he ring me up to tell me about it? He was already well away from the scene of the crime and no one else knew about his rendezvous at the houseboat."

"If he killed her," O'Day said slowly, "his car must have been parked in the lane for near on an hour. He must have known there was a chance someone would have seen it. As you know one of the farm hands reported seeing a car in the lane at about twelve noon."

"I think if it had been a Mercedes he wouldn't have been so vague about the make and so on. Mercedes don't exactly grow on trees around these parts."

"What does a farm hand know about luxury cars, John? But that's not the only thing." The superintendent picked up his memo pad and flicked back through the pages. "Point number one: he said he had never met Brooks before that night he telephoned the AA from her place. If that was so why did he pick 'The Hotbed' to phone from, of all places? There's a call box not a hundred yards away."

Craddock grunted.

"Point number two: he states that when he went to the houseboat on—er—Tuesday the eighteenth he was only there for a short time. Yet we find his fingerprints in the kitchen, on the lavatory seat, in the sitting room—not to mention the bedroom. Point number three: that scratch on his hand. He says he was attacked by a cat. Have you ever heard of a cat attacking humans without provocation? Now, the lab has found minute traces of skin tissue and blood in Brooks's fingernails and it belongs to the same group as Hilton's."

O'Day glanced up at Craddock but the latter was still absorbed in cleaning his pipe.

"Point number four: this boy. That was Hilton's biggest mistake. He was lying wildly to cover the period of time during which the murder was committed. Quite obviously he never expected that we'd go to such lengths to find corroboration of his statement."

"You're not prepared to concede that the boy exists?"

O'Day laughed. "Be your age, John. A grown man, whom we know is going to a date with a seductive woman, lets himself be held up for half an hour climbing trees to rescue a boy's kite."

"There was bark and moss on his clothes."

"That could have been done later, when he realised he'd need an alibi."

"Well, either the crime was premeditated or he killed her in a fit of passion," Craddock pointed out with a flash of spirit. "You can't have it both ways, Tiny."

"I'll settle for one of those alternatives," O'Day said grimly.

Craddock had produced a tin of John Cotton and was prodding more tobacco into his pipe.

"You obviously see some connection between this and the murders you've been following up in Town," he said after he had lit up. "You're not suggesting that Hilton is this 'Mr King' you were telling me about?"

O'Day grimaced slightly and for a moment his thoughts wandered. He stood up, took a little glass tube from his pocket, extracted a pill and swallowed it with a sharp, backward tilt of his head.

"I've no reason to believe so. The fact remains that we know practically nothing about 'Mr King'. All we know is that when the prostitutes were moved off the streets by the new legislation he was the first to realise that there would be more money in it than ever before. His was the first really de luxe call-girl organisation in London and he made a packet out of it. But nobody ever sees 'Mr King'. If they do they keep their mouth shut—or have it shut for them."

"That could have been the motive for the murder of Brooks

also." Craddock was holding the box of matches on top of the bowl of his pipe to improve the draught. "She might have found out too much about 'Mr King' and been blackmailing him. That would explain how she acquired the money to buy the houseboat."

"Yes," O'Day agreed calmly and belched gently behind his hand. "And if she was a professional blackmailer she may have tried to milk friend Hilton—and there's your motive for you."

"You'd never make that stick, Tiny. I don't think you'd get it past the judge, let alone a jury."

"I realise that as well as you do, John. We've a long road to travel yet. In the meantime we haven't enough evidence to hold Hilton. If Jacobs has reported back you can let him go now."

In the waiting room Mike had practically fallen asleep and when Craddock came in to tell him he could go home he was blinking his eyes hard to keep them open.

"Does that mean I'm cleared, Inspector? I mean, I'm free to do what I like?"

"Well, we'd like you to keep in touch with us, Mr Hilton. This investigation is still in its early stages. I hope you aren't contemplating any long journeys, for instance."

Mike looked Craddock in the eye for a few seconds. "I understand," he said quietly. "Until I find that boy I shan't be in the clear. Is that right?"

"Well, if the boy turns up things would be a lot easier for all of us, Mr Hilton."

Mike drove back to 'Tall Trees' with the care of a man who knows he has had a bit too much to drink. He had to keep shaking the sleep out of his head. His brain was far too befuddled to think clearly but in its bemused state it was still capable of registering one inescapable fact. Sel had been murdered and he, Mike Hilton, was being framed as the killer.

When Mike lay down on his couch in the dressing room it was with the idea of resting his eyes and thinking out what his next moves were to be. There was far too much to do to contemplate having the sleep for which his body was craving.

The shrilling of the telephone bell hauled him up from the depths of very deep slumber. He struggled to consciousness with the sense that a considerable period of time had elapsed. The angle of the sunlight slanting in through the window told him that it was already late evening.

He blundered through into the sheeted and curtained double bedroom and grabbed at the white telephone. Before it came to his ear he could hear the repeated pips which indicated that the call was coming from a public box. He waited until the pips stopped and knew the coin had dropped.

"Hello . . . Hilton speaking. Who's there?"

There was a short silence and then the dialling tone started again. The caller, whoever he had been, had hung up. Wrong number, no doubt.

Back in his dressing room he soused his head under the cold tap, washed his teeth to get rid of the foul taste in his mouth and cleaned his eyes out with Optrex. He glanced towards the travelling clock which habitually stood on his dressing table. It wasn't there. Someone had placed it on the bedside table. The hands stood at ten to six. He must have slept for nearly seven hours. But that was not what worried Mike. Looking carefully round the room he saw that a number of small objects were now in slightly different positions. The books by his bed were piled in a different order, his hair brushes were farther apart, the cigarette box and the lighter had changed places. Someone had searched his room and it had not been a thief. Nothing was missing and no thief would have replaced things with such meticulous care.

Had he been too befuddled to notice it when he came in soon before mid-day or had the intruder tiptoed in and gone through his things while he slept?

Ten to six. And he had told Mrs Hall he would be in for lunch. She would be having kittens by now.

He ran quickly downstairs to the dining room. The table was bare. He pushed through the service door to the kitchen. It was tidy and rather colder than usual.

"Mrs Hall?"

The ticking of the kitchen clock was the only response. He walked along the small corridor to the door of her room and knocked sharply on it.

"Mrs Hall? Are you there?"

With some trepidation he turned the handle and pushed the door open. He was met by the faintly musty smell which some people exude in sleep. The drawers of the chest and the doors of the cupboard were open. The sheets and blankets had been neatly folded and piled on the middle of the bed.

Mike closed the door. Rubbing his sticking plaster, which was throbbing slightly, he went back to the hall. Oddly enough, what he resented most was the politeness he had wasted on her. He would have liked to have had just one chance to be really rude to the miserable little bitch.

Damn her tidiness! There was no sign of any food lying about in the kitchen. He investigated the cupboards but discovered that they were either locked or contained crockery. All that he could find was a tin of sweet corn and when he cut his finger on the opener he threw the whole thing away and went storming out of the house.

He got as far as the door of his London club before he

began to hesitate. It was the caption on the newspaper vendor's bill which gave him pause. 'Man questioned in pig-tail murder.' No doubt it was because she did not want to have her good name sullied by contact with a man who got his name into such a story that Mrs Hall had walked out on him. Now Mike realised with a sudden nasty shock that whether or not he was considered guilty of the murder of Selby Brooks the world would judge and condemn him on another count— that of going to an assignation with a woman who was now shown to have a very dubious reputation. Mike felt that he could not face the curious stares or perhaps even the open hostility which he would encounter in the club.

He started the car up again and drove back to the King's Road. For the first time in his life he ate dinner in a Wimpy bar. 'The Four Poster' was a couple of hundred yards up the street. He left the car parked where it was and walked the short distance.

At seven twenty on a Sunday evening 'The Four Poster' had scarcely warmed up. There were about half a dozen people in the saloon bar. At the counter a man in a tweed jacket and grey trousers was crouched on a stool. His age was about thirty and he seemed to have all the time in the world for his pint of mild. His face was spare and watchful, the toecaps of his shoes brightly polished. When the door opened to admit Mike his eyes flicked up to the mirror above the bar to take a swift mental photograph of the newcomer.

Mike hardly noticed him. He went straight to the bar, behind which a young woman with a receding chin and protruding bust was polishing glasses. She finished a glass at her leisure and then looked up at Mike with impersonal eyes.

"Yes?"

"Good-evening," Mike forced politeness into his voice. "I'd like a word with Mr West, please."

The false eyelashes flicked upwards as she shot him a look of wary surprise. She hesitated a second before answering.

"He's not here."

"Well, do you know where I could find him? It's very important."

"Mr West's gone away. I couldn't say where he is exactly."

"How long is he going to be away?"

"I don't know, I'm sure."

"He must have given you some idea. Who's he left in charge of this place?"

"The owners are sending in a new manager tomorrow. In the meantime if you want to make any complaints —"

Her voice was rising and the Chelsea accent was giving way to Stepney.

"I've no complaints," Mike said soothingly. "I just hoped he could give me some information. Perhaps you can help me. Did you know Miss Brooks?"

"Brooks?"

"Yes. She had a room here—until last Tuesday anyway."

"I don't know anything about her," the barmaid said hastily. She picked up a glass and started polishing it furiously. "I only got took on last Friday."

"I see," Mike said, biting on his lower lip. "Well, you might as well give me a gin and french now I'm here."

"Gin and french." Relieved to be on familiar ground, she picked up a small glass and held it under the upturned bottle of Gordon's.

Mike reached into his pocket for a cigarette and glanced up at the mirror behind the bar. A couple who had been sitting in one of the alcoves had stood up and were heading for the door. There was something hasty and furtive about their movements. They were an ill-assorted pair. The woman was well into middle age, plump and floridly dressed. The man accompanying her could not have been much more than twenty. He was wearing a sort of khaki smock stained with paint. He made the mistake of stealing a glance at Mike's back as they went past. It was the drooping Edwardian moustache which gave him away.

Mike swung round from the bar. "Good-evening. I think we've met before."

They stopped and stared at him as if he were a traffic warden.

"I'm Mike Hilton. You remember? We met at Sel's party."

The dawning recognition was overdone, especially by Ruby, who all through her stage career had been prone to overact.

"Why Mike, yes, I didn't recognize you. What brings you here?"

"I wanted to see Bob West. There're a few things I have to ask him but it seems that he's—not at home. Perhaps you can help me."

"We're late already, ducks," Ruby assured him earnestly. Her eyes slid away from him towards Chris Benson. "Chris and I are taking in a film and it's due to start any minute. So if you don't mind —"

She started to push past him. Mike grasped her arm. The flesh felt hard and muscular, almost like a man's.

"I'm sorry, Ruby, but I've got to talk to you."

She glanced appealingly at Chris, but he had seized his opportunity to duck past Mike and get to the door.

"I'll go ahead and see if I can pick up a cab," he muttered and disappeared through the swing door. Ruby's eyes, which had followed him with frustrated rage, swung back defiantly to Mike.

"Come and sit down, Ruby. I'll buy you a drink."

"I don't want any drink," Ruby snapped. "I told you. I haven't got time." All the same she let Mike seat her at one of the tables in the middle of the room. From his stool by the bar the lean man with the watchful eyes was taking in the whole scene. With a glance over his shoulder in that direction, Mike leaned over the table.

"You've got to tell me about Sel," he said in a low voice. "Do you know whether . . ."

"I don't want to talk about Sel." Ruby's mouth had started to quiver. "It upsets me."

"Ruby, you've got to talk about her. There are some things I must know."

"I was very upset about Sel. Very." She began to sniff and fumbled in her handbag for a handkerchief. "The police already asked me a lot of questions. Had the nerve to come round and walk into my place as if they were the bailiffs. But you know all about that, don't you?"

"No." Mike shook his head, meeting her accusing gaze.

"Didn't you put them up to it?"

"No, of course I didn't."

"Didn't you tell them I was a friend of hers?"

"I didn't have to, Ruby. They seemed to know a good deal about this place already."

Ruby gave Mike a long look of remarkable astuteness. Evidently she decided to believe him. She put her elbows on the table and leant towards him. Her stale breath was slightly perfumed by a whiff of gin.

"What is it you want to know?"

"Is it true that Sel was the owner of that houseboat?"

"Is that what she told you?"

"Was she the owner?"

Ruby hesitated a little before nodding her head. "Yes."

"Now, have you any idea where she got the money to buy it?"

"What business is that of yours?"

108

"Quite a lot. The police suggested that she was not above trying a little blackmail and that possibly —"

"Did she blackmail *you*?" Ruby demanded fiercely.

"She lied to me. She must have done, because —"

"Did she blackmail you?" Ruby repeated in a lower but more insistent tone.

"Well, no. She didn't —"

"Did she borrow money from you?"

"No."

"Did she even try to borrow money from you?"

"Well, no." Instinctively Mike had leaned back, partly to escape the blast of Ruby's breath and partly because she looked almost ready to scratch his eyes out.

"Then what the hell are you bellyaching about? Judge people as you find them."

Before he could recover from his astonishment she had stood up and flounced out through the door. Mike thoughtfully stubbed his cigarette out in the Cinzano ashtray and pushed his chair back. He finished off the remains of his gin and french and went towards the door.

"Excuse me, sir," the barmaid called. There was a faint undertone of triumph in her voice. "I don't think you paid for your drink."

"Neither I did," Mike said. She pursed her lips and would not look at him as he moved in embarrassment towards the bar. "How much do I owe you?"

"That's three and three, please."

Mike put two florins on the counter and turned away. "That's all right."

She did not say thanks. The man on the stool finished his pint of mild, put down one and tenpence. He waited till Mike had gone out into the King's Road before slipping off his stool and casually walking after him.

It had been a gloomy Sunday. To take his mind off his own troubles Mike had followed the example of Ruby and Chris and turned in at a cinema. It was a film about the second war, made by a brilliant young director, and its purpose was to show that all the British generals were corrupt and most of the soldiers cowardly or brutal. Watching it Mike reflected that Truth is the final casualty in every conflict.

Some vaguely defined hope took him back to 'Tall Trees' for the night. Yet as he drove up the avenue the dark and empty house seemed to repulse him. When he opened the front door and entered the hall, tiptoeing so as not to smash the silence, the dim interior seemed to be peopled with ghosts —Jill's, Ruth's, his own.

He read in bed till the book slid from his fingers and clattered to the floor. When he woke in the morning the bedside light was still on. Down in the kitchen he managed finally to locate the ingredients of a scratch breakfast. It was a relief in the end to escape from the listening house.

On the way into Town he stopped at Chatsworth's garage and made the excuse of filling up with petrol. Usually Chatsworth strolled out from his glass-fronted office to pass the time of day. This morning he seemed to be so absorbed in his mail that he had not seen the Mercedes. When he had paid the attendant Mike ran his car forward a few yards and then got out again. He went to the window of the office, and rapped on it with his knuckles. Chatsworth glanced up, simulating surprise, and then smiled. Mike pushed open the door.

"Morning, Colin."

"Morning, Mike. Not trouble again, I hope."

"Not car trouble this time. Can you spare a few minutes?"

"Well, actually we've got a bit of a flap on this morning," Chatsworth said defensively. "But sit ye down. What can I do for you?"

Deliberately ignoring the other man's slightly cold manner Mike sat down in the easy chair provided for customers. He noted that Chatsworth had not been too busy to study the morning paper. It lay open at the side of his desk. Featured prominently on the front page was a photograph of the houseboat with inset photographs of Selby Brooks and Mike.

"I don't have to tell you, Colin, that I'm in a bit of a spot."

"I know, old boy. Very sorry about it. Anything I can do to help —"

"Colin, you remember that morning when I left the Mercedes to have the wing repaired and you lent me a Morris Thousand?"

"Yup." Chatsworth slid back in his seat, put the tips of his fingers together and watched Mike over the top of them with a curious expression.

"You were talking to a tall bloke in a check suit. I seem to recall that you were trying to sell him an Austin Healey."

"Oh, you mean Barry," Chatsworth answered at once. "Barry Freeman. Very tall chap with horn-rimmed spectacles."

"That's him. Do you know where he lives?"

"Haven't a clue. I do a fair amount of business with him, and from time to time we hit the town together but I've never been to his home. Come to think of it he's never even referred to where he lives. Shouldn't think he sleeps there much. He's a terrible woman-chaser."

"Oh." Mike pursed his lips, unable to hide his disappointment.

"All I can tell you," Chatsworth went on, "is that he has a site of about four acres where he keeps about five hundred cars in various stages of wreckage. He's well known in the trade as someone you can unload junk on. He sells the better ones, breaks up others for spares and crushes the write-offs for resale as scrap metal. Doesn't do too badly, I would say."

"Where is this place?"

"Somewhere out near Aylesbury. But the chances are a hundred to one against you finding him there. He's always on the move, going round looking at stuff he's been offered. Why, are you thinking of doing a swap?"

Chatsworth's tone was bantering. He nodded at the Mercedes, visible through the wide plate-glass window.

"Good heavens, no! I think perhaps he might be able to help me."

"In what way?"

"He knew Sel —"

"Sel?"

"Selby Brooks. The girl on the front page of your newspaper. You've just been reading about her—and me."

"Oh." Trying to hide his embarrassment Chatsworth nervously fingered the newspaper. "Well, that doesn't completely surprise me. Old Barry knows most people. He gets around. Actually I'm seeing him tonight. I could ask him to give you a ring."

"Is he coming down here?"

"No. I've taken in an M.G. in part exchange. I happen to know it's clapped out so I can't offer it to any of my customers. I'll see what Barry will offer. We're going to kill two birds with one stone." Chatsworth chuckled at some secret joke. "I'm meeting him up in town."

Mike had stood up. A very amateur driver was trying to manœuvre his car up to the air line and had already almost scraped the side of the Mercedes.

"Would you mind if I came along?"

Chatsworth stopped grinning and became suddenly serious, his brow furrowed and he ran his tongue over his upper lip.

"Well—if you'd like to—sure. Come along."

"Thanks very much," Mike said before the other could change his mind. "Where shall I meet you?"

"Come along here about nine. We can go up together."

Mike had already decided to brazen it out and go to the office that day. To stay away, he felt, would have amounted to a confession of guilt. To his great surprise the female secretarial staff were looking at him as if he were some kind of film or television hero rather than a suspected criminal. Girls who had formerly ignored him seemed to be resting their eyes on him for longer than usual. Even some of the male staff went out of their way to nod to him or make a friendly remark.

His first move was to seek an interview with old Robbo, the patriarch of the firm. You could never quite tell what Robbo was thinking. He placed Mike in his big armchair and walked up and down in front of him while he told his story. He did not interrupt or make any comment until Mike came to the words he had carefully prepared: ". . . to offer you my resignation. In the best interests of the firm . . ."

"Stop!" L. R. Robinson had abruptly ceased his pacing. He was facing Mike with uplifted hand. "I don't want to hear another word about resignation. You have done exactly what I hoped you would do. You have come in here and told me the whole story. Mike, I have known you since you were a boy and I do not think you would tell me an untruth. You say that you are innocent of this crime and I implicitly believe you. That you have been indiscreet I will not deny. But I realise that you have been distressed by Ruth's leaving you and in such circumstances men may be forgiven for—well, seeking consolation elsewhere."

"I wish the police felt the same as you do, sir."

"The police don't know you, I do. If there's any help we can give you . . ."

113

"I may need a little time off. Somehow I feel that if I am to get out of this mess it will be by my own efforts."

The 'Nudeville' club was more luxurious than most of the strip joints that have broken out over Soho. Its entrance was as pretentious and well lit as a small, rather select cinema. While Colin signed Mike in as a 'member' and paid their admission money Mike found his eyes irresistibly caught by the photographs of women displayed at the entrance.

"Come on," Chatsworth called to him. "You'll see something better than that inside."

Mike followed his host down a flight of stairs into a plushy, thickly-carpeted bar where the lights were low and the music hushed. The ebony tables and the black leather armchairs were mostly occupied by well dressed middle aged men, many of them business groups up from the country for some commercial jamboree. Chatsworth glanced round the room and led Mike to the bar, behind which reigned a tall blonde girl.

"Evening, Peg," Chatsworth greeted her with easy familiarity. "No sign of Mr Freeman yet?"

"He was here not a moment ago. He may have gone through to watch the show." She nodded towards a curtained doorway through which Mike caught a glimpse of velvety arc lights slicing the blue haze of cigarette smoke, and the corner of a stage from which flesh and sequins gleamed.

"Well, give us a couple of large whiskies—on the rocks."

Peg turned her back to measure out the drinks and Mike quickly switched his gaze to the luminous panels above the bar. Each one featured a naked girl in a different posture.

After a little while Mike dragged his eyes away from the panel.

"You come here often?"

114

"Pretty often," Chatsworth answered absently. "Where's Doris tonight, Peg?"

"She caught a cold. I told her often enough about putting her sweater on when she goes out the back but she won't be told. You can't do this job if you've got the sneezes."

"Too true," Chatsworth agreed. "And a summer cold is the devil to shake off."

He gave Mike a wink and Mike smiled nervously back. From the darkened room beyond the curtains came the sound of scattered applause. A moment later they parted as a group of men came out. Among them was a tall man wearing a slightly shiny light-weight suit with a striped bow tie.

"Ah, here's the man himself." Chatsworth raised a hand to greet Freeman, who came towards them, his eyes flicking from Chatsworth to Mike and back again. "Evening, Barry. I think you know Mike Hilton."

When Freeman turned towards him Mike was unable to interpret his expression. The heavy frames of his spectacles masked his eyes.

"We met on the pavement outside 'The Four Poster' the other night. The night of Selby Brooks's party."

"Oh, yes. I'm afraid I was a bit high. Hope I didn't say anything I shouldn't. Glad to meet you again."

He put a hand out and Mike shook it. The flesh of Freeman's hand was hard and dry and surprisingly cold.

"Selby was quite a friend of yours, I understand. I was very sorry to hear about that terrible business. It must have been an awful shock for you—finding her like that."

His expression was a mixture of sympathy and curiosity. He studied Mike for a moment then turned to Chatsworth.

"You've brought the M.G.?"

"Yes. I found a parking space just round the corner. But Mike here wants to ask you something first. Another whisky

115

please, Peg." Chatsworth nodded at Freeman to show that the whisky was for him. "I'll be with you in a moment," he said to his two companions. "I just want to have a look at this new French girl. I'm told she's a real heat-wave."

Freeman watched Chatsworth's back till he went through the curtain.

"Well, what was it you wanted to know, old boy?"

"I—er—thought you might be able to help me —" Mike began, wondering how to broach the subject with Freeman.

"Of course. Any pal of Colin's —"

"You knew Selby, didn't you?"

Freeman turned away for a moment to take the whisky which Peg had placed on the counter for him. "Thanks, Peg." He took a sip from the rapidly misting glass, looking quizzically at Mike over the rim. "Yes, I knew her. Not very well, though."

"Do you mind my asking—how well?"

Freeman glanced over his shoulder at the man who had come to the bar beside him. He moved a little nearer to Mike and lowered his voice. "One night only, old boy. But what a night! Then a chum whispered something in my ear and you couldn't see my heels for dust."

"When was this?" Mike was persisting with his questioning, despite the fact that every answer seemed to drive the nails deeper into his coffin. To think that he'd actually fallen for that line of Sel's about being 'irresistibly attractive to women'. All the time she must have been laughing up her sleeve at him.

"Oh, six or seven months ago," Freeman was saying. "Perhaps longer."

"And what did this chum of yours whisper?"

"He told me she made her living by indulging in a spot of judicious blackmail. You know—photographs of respectable

116

chaps in kinky situations. That was enough for me. I don't mind paying for my pleasure but there's a limit."

Mike felt the blood come flushing to his cheeks. "All the same you came to her party the other night —"

Freeman smiled foolishly and held up his drink to illustrate the point. "Same old trouble as usual. I was full to the scalp that night. Bumped into Ingrid—you know, that Swedish kid I was with. She said there was this party she'd been invited to and insisted on my taking her along. As soon as I realised it was in the old 'Hotbed' I was out of there as fast as my little rubber legs would carry me."

Freeman shook his head and grinned wryly.

"What about Bob West? Sel told me —"

"Bob West? Who's he?"

"The landlord of 'The Four Poster'. Late landlord, I should say. He seems to have hopped it."

"If he's the chap who used to serve behind the bar I've only met him once or twice. Don't know anything about him, old man."

"Sel told me he was her uncle."

"She did?" Freeman finished his whisky and looked around for Peg. "Same again, please, Peg. And set one up for Mr Chatsworth too. He'll need cooling off after he's got an eyeful of that new girl."

He slid a flat gold cigarette case from his pocket, offered one to Mike and lit up with a lighter which appeared as if by magic from his fob pocket.

"If you ask me, old man," he said confidentially, "all these kids are told exactly what to say and what not to say. And if they put a foot wrong —" He drew a finger over his throat and bared his teeth at Mike. "I've been around quite a bit but I'm not rugged enough to get mixed up in that kind of racket."

"You think Sel was part of—I mean you think that she was working under someone's instructions?"

"Well, what do you think? Sel, Ingrid, Vida, Iris—all those kids. Someone's running them all right and he doesn't stand for any nonsense. Look what happened to that other youngster. What was her name? Della something-or-other."

"I don't know who you mean." Mike picked up one of the whiskies which Peg had put on the counter. He was beginning to be glad he had left his car at Chatsworth's garage. If the evening went on like this he would not be in a fit state to drive.

"It was in all the papers. She used to be one of the regulars at 'The Hotbed'. Then she kicked over the traces, gave up tarting and became a stripper. That was all right but instead of keeping her mouth shut —" Again Freeman pursed his lips and shook his head. "She was murdered at the very door of a member of the vice squad."

"Oh, I remember now. She was stabbed. Somewhere up near Notting Hill Gate."

"That's right. You've got it, old boy. Notting Hill Gate. Damn funny business that. Damn funny altogether."

He glanced across the bar. Peg had stopped arranging glasses and was standing perfectly still, listening to them. Mike was beginning to feel he had had enough of Freeman's confidences. The man was trying to be helpful, he supposed, but there was something nauseating about the simper which continually lurked about his face when he was talking about these girls.

"But Sel—surely she hadn't anything to do with that affair?"

"I wouldn't be too sure about that, old man. It's a pretty tight little world. All these girls know each other."

He was again studying Mike but the light was still glinting

on his spectacles and Mike could not tell whether his expression was wary or friendly. He took Mike's arm and turned him away from the bar.

"You don't mind if I offer you a little advice, old man? Take my tip and don't dig too deep into all this. Otherwise *you* are liable to end up with a knife in your back."

He gave Mike's arm a slight shake and then released it. Once again a flutter of applause came from the room beyond and Chatsworth pushed his way through the curtains. He looked slightly dazed.

"Well, Colin. Did she come up to scratch?"

"Phew." Chatsworth shook his head like a surfacing dog. "I need a whisky."

"There's one on the counter for you. But knock it back quick. I want to have a look at this heap you've brought for me."

Chapter Eight

In the end Mike had to take a taxi back to Chatsworth's garage to pick up his car. Freeman had offered a price for the M.G. and Chatsworth had sold it there and then for cash. Mike refused the invitation to help spend the proceeds. Chatsworth was one of those people who are very much affected by the company they are in and Freeman seemed to bring out the silliest side of him. Mike made some excuse and parted from them at the door of a gambling club.

As he drove up the avenue to 'Tall Trees' he saw that a light was burning in the hall. The sun had been shining brightly when he went out and he must have failed to notice that it was on. He put the car in the garage and walked along the 'cloister', feeling in his pocket for his keys.

Once inside the hall he stopped. It is curious how a human presence betrays itself. Mike knew instinctively that someone had come into the house since he'd left, might even still be here. He remembered the signs of a furtive intruder in his dressing room, the unidentified caller who had hung up the phone as soon as he answered.

His rubber-soled shoes made no noise as he prowled round the ground floor of the house, checking the windows and the garden door. They were all well secured. In the larder another light had been left on, but he could have done that himself when he was getting his breakfast. He stood for a minute looking at the coffee cup on the draining board, trying to remember whether he had washed it up that morning. If he had the intruder had taken time off to brew himself a hot drink.

He used the extreme edge of the stairs to move up to the first floor so as to eliminate creaks and stood for a few seconds on the top step, listening. Somewhere on the first floor a board creaked quietly under the weight of a footfall. With eyes now attuned to the darkness he crept to the door of his dressing room. It was ajar. He pushed it open with his foot, standing well back. The gleam of moonlight from the garden beyond outlined the window clearly. As he went cautiously in he saw the bar of light under the door that connected his dressing room with the double bedroom—Ruth's room.

He needed four strides to reach the door. He took a firm grip of the handle, drew in a deep breath and flung it open. The woman was bending over in front of Ruth's antique chest, doing something to one of the drawers. With a gasp of fright she straightened up and whirled round to face him. Bunched for attack Mike checked himself and unclenched his fists.

They stood, staring at each other without a word for ten seconds. Then Mike opened his mouth to say something, but no words came. In the end it was she who broke the tension.

"What happened to Mrs Hall?"

"She just walked out. Didn't even leave a message. Frightened for her good name, I expect."

"Typical. Who's been looking after you—doing your breakfast and so forth?"

"I have. Spent most of the time trying to find where things are. I thought you were in Paris."

"I was—until after dinner this evening. I was lucky to get a seat on the last Air France flight. That's one advantage of working for the company."

They were both embarrassed and trying to cover it with this banal conversation, as if they'd been separated for a mere five minutes.

"You must be tired. Can I get you a drink or something?"

She shook her head. She was wearing a new suit which he had not seen before. She must have bought it in Paris. Somehow it made her look slimmer and a little taller. Her hair was done a new way too. An open suitcase was on the bed, half unpacked.

"No, I don't need a drink."

"Why have you come back, Ruth?"

"Don't you know why? I bought a copy of the *Express* this afternoon. When I read the story I realised that the whole thing was really my fault. You didn't expect me to leave you to face this alone?"

Mike was still in the doorway. Ruth had not moved from her position by the chest but he realised that she was restraining herself. The ball was in his court. Some instinct told him that unless he made the right move now—at the very beginning of this new relationship—the chance would be gone for ever.

"Ruth." He went towards her and drew her into his arms. She came to him yieldingly. She was comfortingly solid in his grasp, a woman a man could anchor himself to. Her fingers gently caressing the nape of his neck were immeasurably soothing. The memory of Sel's feline suppleness flashed into his mind, twisting the tail of his conscience.

"There, there, darling," Ruth was whispering in his ear. "It'll be all right now. Everything will be all right now."

"And do you think you were really falling in love with her?"

"I think I was smitten rather than in love. She'd literally

122

turned my head. Something was happening to my chemistry that I couldn't control."

They were sitting in the sun parlour, drinking coffee and watching the shadows in the moonlit garden. The hour since Mike had returned home had flown by. He'd taken the plunge and told Ruth the whole story, even down to the afternoon he'd spent with Sel on the houseboat. Her reaction had astonished him. She had listened with rapt attention, almost inquisitiveness. She kept shooting him glances as if she were seeing him for the first time. In an odd way he had begun to feel that they were closer to each other than at any time since their marriage.

"But you did not tell the police about—this love-making."

"No."

"Why didn't you? It might be dangerous to conceal something as important as that."

"They made everything I told them sound so stupid. This didn't seem to affect the issue and I just couldn't bear to have them prying into the details. Especially as I'd changed my mind about spending the week-end on the houseboat."

"Had you?"

"Yes. I'd left my suitcase in the boot of the car."

"But from what I can gather the police haven't accepted your story."

"No. And when I think about it I can't blame them. I mean it does sound rather silly. I have a date with this girl for which I set off about half an hour too early. Then I'm late because I've helped a boy recover his kite."

"What sort of age was he?"

"About nine, I would say. I'm not very good at judging children's ages."

Ruth reached over to put her empty coffee cup down on the ceramic-topped table. "If we'd had a son he might have been just about that age."

"You see, once I'd undertaken to get his kite down for him, I couldn't just give up and admit defeat, could I? I'd have been letting him down. If you could have seen the look in his eyes —"

"I can understand that, Mike. There's still something of the boy in you, and you never were one to admit defeat."

Ruth stood up and moved round to collect Mike's cup and place it on the tray with her own. It had been a relief to drink proper coffee after the muck the percolator had produced for him.

"I wish I could make the police see it that way," Mike sighed. "Sometimes I begin to wonder whether this boy exists at all—whether I dreamt the whole episode."

"Don't be absurd," Ruth reprimanded him briskly. "Of course he exists. If he was on the common on his own he must be a local boy."

"Well, I searched that whole area, Ruth. Even the police haven't been able to find him. If he exists why hasn't he turned up?"

Ruth had picked the tray up and was standing gazing down at him. She was looking determined and slightly stern.

"Your alibi really depends on finding this boy. Is that right, Mike?"

Mike nodded.

"Well then, if the police can't find him we will!"

That was Monday night, or rather early Tuesday morning. At ten o'clock Mike telephoned old Robbo to inform him firstly that Ruth was back and secondly that he needed several days off.

Ruth had harnessed her very considerable organising ability to the search. She had bought an Ordnance Survey map of the district and drawn a series of circles with the common at Chapel Denning as the centre. Using the yellow pages

124

of the local telephone directory she had listed every organisation which had to do with young people—schools, youth clubs, welfare and care organisations, even the probation officers. As a first measure Mike drove her to Chapel Denning and showed her the actual tree which he had climbed.

"You mean to tell me you climbed out along that branch? You must be crazy."

All the same, he thought he detected admiration in the glance she gave him.

"Which direction did he make off in?"

"Straight across the common." Mike pointed towards the houses about half a mile away. "I've tried every house in Chapel Denning, don't worry."

"And nobody came past while you were scrambling about in this tree? I mean if we can't find the boy someone else might be able to corroborate your story."

"I don't think anything came past. Most of the traffic goes along the roads that lead to the village. You'd only come this way if you were swanning around, killing time."

"Right. Then we'll extend the area," Ruth said briskly. "Today we'll try everything within a mile radius. Tomorrow we'll extend it to two and so on."

As the days went by Mike grew heartily sick of the sight of the rising generation. He watched hordes of children darting about on their school playgrounds during the morning break, scanned the lines of children waiting to see the special film shows put on at local cinemas, studied well-behaved little communities of children from broken homes, watched the pastimes organised at youth clubs in the evening. There were scores of nine-year-old boys with steel-rimmed spectacles, there were dozens who wore a metal plate on their upper teeth, there were hundreds with tousled curly hair, but none of them had the wistfully appealing eyes of the boy he had seen on the common.

After the third day Ruth began to go systematically round the undertakers. She'd hit on the idea that the boy had met with an accident, or been taken suddenly ill and died. The result was the same — a complete blank.

One evening after they'd gone round the children's wards in all the local hospitals they went into a main road hotel for a drink. Mike saw the dining room menu on the bar and thought it looked promising.

"Let's have dinner," he suggested. "Looks as if the food here's pretty good."

Ruth nodded.

He thought that she was at last beginning to look tired and dispirited. She'd thrown herself into the search with such confident energy, but now even she was beginning to show the first signs of defeatism.

"I can never thank you enough for this, Ruth," he said. "Even though we haven't found him it's been such a relief to feel that I've been *doing* something, instead of just waiting for the police to weave a web around me. I wish O'Day wasn't so inhuman."

O'Day had hauled Mike in for a further session of questioning the previous day. Somehow or other he had found evidence that Mike's visit to the houseboat on Tuesday the eighteenth had not been as platonic as he had made out. In the end Mike had admitted how intimate his relations with Selby Brooks had been.

"Why did you withhold this information in your earlier statement, Mr Hilton?" he had asked with tart disapproval.

"I didn't see that it had any bearing on the murder."

"I think that we are the best judge of that. In point of fact you were asked a perfectly straight question and you chose to give an untruthful answer. That was unwise, Mr Hilton. It lays the whole of your statement open to question."

"There must be some areas of human relationships which even the police respect," Mike retorted. "Aren't you prepared to make any concessions to privacy?"

"Not where murder is concerned. When a crime has sexual characteristics anyone who has sexual relations with the victim must be suspect."

He hadn't told Ruth exactly what had passed between him and the superintendent at that meeting. Even so her attitude to the police was not sympathetic.

"If they'd spend less time trying to find evidence against you and more helping to find this boy —"

Mike's instinct for good eating places had not failed him. They were given an excellent meal in the hotel dining room, which they ate sitting side by side on a bench seat against the wall. From their position they could watch the other diners and compare impressions of them. As the coffee was brought he felt her hand resting on his knee and put his own on top of it. When he looked round at her he found her eyes fixed on him with an expression he had not seen since the days of their engagement. In the heavily shaded light her features were softened. Her hand had turned over in his grasp and their fingers were enmeshed. He felt a strange physical excitement passing through his limbs. Something had happened to Ruth. Her whole manner, even the feel of her hand, was different. Her personality had reawakened, her body had come alive again. Was it because of some experience she had had in Paris — or was it a strange by-product of his affair with Selby?

The truth, if Mike had been wise enough to perceive it, was much simpler. Ruth was a woman who had to be needed. While Mike was successful, athletically and commercially, he did not arouse her womanly protectiveness. The death of Jill had killed an instinct in her which Mike had not been able to awaken till he had proved himself weak, erring and in need.

He drove home from the hotel slowly, not because he was frightened of police traps, but to spin out this precious closeness for as long as possible. It was well after ten when he turned into the drive of 'Tall Trees'. The white painted fencing gleamed briefly in the headlights as he swung the car round towards the garage. The wind had blown the door shut, pushing it past the stone which Mike had left to prop it open.

"All right," Ruth said, opening her door. "I'll do it."

She slid out and he dipped his headlights so as not to dazzle her as she pulled the door open. Then he flipped them up again and let in the clutch. The Mercedes was halfway into the garage when Mike braked sharply.

Ruth peered in through the rear window at him. He was sitting stock still in the seat staring at the wall in front of him.

"What's the matter, darling?"

He had not heard her. He opened the door on the driver's side and stepped out, still staring at the garage wall.

"Ruth! Take a look at this!"

She squeezed past the side of the car and looked over his shoulder.

"What is it, Mike?"

His answer was to nod towards the wall, where a tyre had been suspended from a hook to form a buffer in case the car ran too far forward. On the protruding end of this hook had been stuck a child's kite.

Mike went forward, his shadow cast hugely on the wall by the headlights. He took the kite down and turned it over in his hands.

"Someone has a weird sense of humour," Ruth remarked.

"I don't know about humour." Mike was staring at the kite with a bewildered expression. "But I do know it's the same kite! It's the same one, Ruth!"

'The Pig-tail Murder', as the newspaper reporters had christened it, had moved off the front page several days before. Reading the City news next morning Mike had made up his mind that he ought to go and put in a day at the office. Share prices were falling and the stock market was in a state of uncertainty.

"I may be in a spot myself," he told Ruth, "but I can't let my clients down."

"I thought you said Hartley was looking after them for you."

"Yes, he is. But it's not quite the same thing. Anyway we might as well face it. We've nothing to show for the last few days' work."

"Except a kite," Ruth pointed out.

Mike finished off his coffee and reached for the cigarette box.

"The kite by itself doesn't tell us much. I'll take it in to Craddock on the way into town. I only hope I don't bump into O'Day. He'd probably suspect me of buying a kite and planting it there myself."

"I think the kite tells us quite a lot," Ruth said. She had pushed her breakfast plate aside and drawn a fresh cup of coffee in front of her. Now she had her elbows on the table and was cradling the cup in both hands.

"Such as what?"

"As I see it this confirms that the reason why the boy has not come to light is connected with the murder. It means that the boy has told someone about meeting you and that someone realises who you are. It means that we are being watched by someone who is anxious to keep us on tenterhooks and stop us

E

losing interest in the search. And my guess is it's the same person as is trying to pin the blame on you."

Mike looked at her thoughtfully through his cigarette smoke. "And they came to this house last night while we were out."

Ruth nodded. "They may even have been watching us when we came back. Several times lately I've had the feeling that we were being followed. I've noticed the same car cruising along behind us even after we'd taken several turnings. Three or four times I've been almost sure I've seen the same man hanging about near places we've visited."

"But what on earth would be the point of that? I think you must be imagining things."

Mike spoke with emphasis, but all the same he could not help remembering the warning Barry Freeman had given him in the 'Nudeville' club.

They both started when the telephone bell shrilled sharply behind them.

"I'll answer it," Mike said, pushing his chair back. "You finish your coffee."

There was a telephone extension just inside the doorway to the sun parlour, where they were having breakfast. Mike picked up the receiver and said, "Hello." Since the murder he had given up his usual procedure of announcing his identity straight away.

Once again he heard the repeated pips which indicate that a call is coming through from a coin box. He waited, half expecting to hear the dialling tone which would indicate that the caller, having obtained an answer, would ring off.

This time, however, he heard a man's voice.

"I want to speak to Mr Hilton, please." The voice was muffled. Mike had to press the receiver close to his ear to hear him.

"Who wants to speak to him?"

"It doesn't matter who. Just fetch Mr Hilton for me. Tell him it's important."

Mike hesitated for only a second. "This is Hilton speaking. Now, who are you?"

"Just listen carefully," the voice went on. "You found the kite?"

Mike knocked on the glass partition to attract Ruth's attention and signalled frantically to her to go and listen to the conversation in the hall. She got the message at once, and bustled past him.

"I asked you if you found the kite," the caller was saying petulantly.

"Yes. I found it."

"Now you'd like to find the boy, wouldn't you?"

"What's that? I didn't quite catch what you said."

"Now you'd like to find the boy, wouldn't you?" The words were repeated more loudly but with exactly the same inflection, as if the caller was reciting a lesson. There was the faintest click as Ruth picked up the receiver in the hall.

"Yes." The strain under which Mike had been living was evident from the pitch of his voice. "Of course I'd like to find him."

"Then meet me this morning."

"But who is that? Who is it speaking?"

"I'll see you at twelve thirty—and don't mention this to anyone, because if you do —"

"I shan't mention it to anyone," Mike said quickly. "But who are you? Where are you speaking from?"

"Do you know Dubinsky's bookshop?"

"Dubinsky's bookshop? No —"

"It's in Chelsea. On the King's Road about two hundred yards from 'The Four Poster'. I'll see you there at twelve thirty—sharp."

"Yes," Mike said slowly. "Yes, all right. But look here, hadn't you better give me your name otherwise how will I know —"

Suddenly the dialling tone was buzzing in his ear. He realised that the caller had put his instrument down.

"Did you hear that?" he asked Ruth, speaking loudly over the dialling tone.

Her voice came back to him down the line.

"Yes. I don't know which of you was more unsure of himself—the voice or you."

"You think he was frightened?"

"Yes. Scared out of his wits."

"I'd forgotten how nice your voice sounded on the telephone," Mike said.

"Does it? You should ring me up more often."

Dubinsky's bookshop was sandwiched between a greengrocer, who used his produce as a cubist artist uses paints, and a men's 'boutique' displaying the latest in male wearing apparel. Second-hand books of the cheaper variety had been crammed into the racks which stood outside the shop. Behind the small panes of the ancient window had been propped a few selected rare volumes with their pages held open to show the antique printing.

Inside, the walls were covered from floor to ceiling with shelves. At the back of the shop a door led through to a smaller room where, in locked cabinets, Dubinsky kept the books which he would show to customers who enquired whether he had any erotica for sale. A large free-standing bookshelf, with battalions of volumes raged on either side, had been placed across the back end of the shop, concealing the entrance to the inner room and forming a dark narrow corridor between itself and the wall. It contained largely theological works, and

132

Dubinsky had cynically christened this shadowy corridor 'the cloister'.

Perched on a pair of steps inside 'the cloister' Chris Benson was laboriously removing a volume at a time from the shelf, dusting it and putting it back again. By peering through the tops of the less lofty volumes he could see the face of the old grandfather clock which ticked the minutes away for the benefit of tomes older than itself. The long hand was just jerking up to the tenth minute after mid-day. Dubinsky was seated behind his riotously untidy desk at the side of the shop just inside the door. He had a pair of scissors in his hand and was cutting a sheet of cartridge paper into strips.

A girl who had been browsing along the racks of books outside came in with a Galsworthy in her hand. She walked up to the front of Dubinsky's desk.

"I'll take this one."

He flashed his rimless spectacles up at her, took the book and glanced at the price written inside the cover.

"Three and six, please."

She handed him two half-crowns. He opened a drawer, took out a shilling and a sixpence, placed them on top of the book and slid it towards her.

"Thank you. Good morning."

"Good morning," Dubinsky said, thoughtfully watching her stern as she walked to the door. "Come again, please."

Chris had climbed down from his ladder, and by the time the girl made her exit was standing by Dubinsky's desk.

"You get off if you like, Louis. I can manage all right."

The bookseller looked up affectionately at the young man.

"I'll wait till you've been out for lunch. You know these hospitals. I may not be back for hours."

"Makes no difference to me," Chris said, with seeming casualness. "I've got sandwiches anyway."

"Well, in that case . . ." Dubinsky shrugged and got off his chair. He wasn't very much taller standing than sitting down. His trousers were hauled almost up to his armpits by a pair of leather braces. He took the jacket which was hanging over the back of his chair and put it on.

"If it's nothing serious I shouldn't be too long."

"It's nothing serious, Louis. Now don't worry."

"I hope not. Here—you'll need some cigarettes." Dubinsky fished a crumpled packet of Gauloises from his pocket. Chris made a show of refusing them but Dubinsky pressed them on him. "Saw you only had one left. It'll save you going out."

Chris nodded his thanks. Dubinsky gave him a little pat on the back, looked round as if he were forgetting something and went out of the shop. The bell above the door emitted a crisp 'ping' as he opened it.

Left alone Chris glanced again at the clock. Thirteen minutes past. He took a cigarette from the packet and lit it with a match. His fingers were trembling slightly. After a few puffs he balanced it on the ashtray and, sitting down behind the desk, began to carry on with Dubinsky's task of cutting the cartridge paper into strips.

After about a minute the bell pinged. He looked up to see a flushed Ruby Stevenson closing the door. As she did so she looked quickly up and down the foot-path to make sure no one was following her into the shop. She hurried over to the desk, already fumbling at her handbag.

"I thought he was never going. What time is it?" She twisted her neck to look at the clock. "We've still got ten minutes."

She balanced her handbag on the edge of the desk and rummaged inside for an envelope. She handed it across the desk to him. "Here you are, Chris."

134

He stared at the envelope but did not take it. She knew him well enough to interpret the sullen expression on his face.

"For heaven's sake, Chris! You don't want to go on like this, do you? Doing part-time jobs for peanuts?"

Chris pursed his lips, then relented and took the envelope from her. He held it in one hand tapping it against the tops of the fingers of the other. Ruby helped herself to a cigarette from the packet he had left on the table, found a lighter in her bag and blew smoke. There was something rather stylish about her manner of lighting a cigarette.

"You understand"—she nodded at the envelope to emphasise her point. "He mustn't get hold of this. Just let him take a look." Her eyes followed his hand as he picked up his cigarette. The trembling was now unmistakable.

"What if he doesn't play?"

"He'll play all right. Wouldn't you if you were in his shoes?"

"How much did you say to ask?"

"Try six thousand for a start. That'll be three thousand for each of us."

Chris nodded vaguely. He pushed one pale cheek outwards with his tongue. An expression of tenderness flowed into Ruby's puckered eyes. She leant across the desk, seized his hand in hers and squeezed it hard, as if to impart strength to him.

"Don't worry, Chris. Just keep thinking that this time tomorrow we'll be in Paris."

"What do I do when I've seen him?"

"Go back to my flat and wait. You know where I leave the key, don't you?"

Chris nodded absently. His eyes wandered up to the clock.

"Twenty-five past," she said, following his eyes. "I'd best

be going. Don't forget to put the 'Closed' sign up as soon as he comes in."

He was biting the top of a nail as she went out into the King's Road.

When Mike walked into the shop four minutes later its only occupant seemed to be a dark figure, lurking like a vampire under the bookshelves. When he heard the bell ping he glanced round showing Mike an introspective face, pale watery eyes peering out through thick lenses. Mike stared at him fixedly, wondering if this were the owner of the voice. The hands of the clock had just moved past twelve thirty. After a minute the book fancier seemed to become unnerved by Mike's stare. He replaced the book and scuttled towards the door. No sooner had the bell emitted its customary ping than Chris emerged from 'the cloister'.

"Good-morning, Mr Hilton."

Mike spun round at the slightly over-dramatised greeting. His eyes followed Chris in astonishment as the young man, giving him a wide berth, skirted past him and made for the door. When he got there he shot a bolt and reversed the cardboard sign, so that the word 'Open' was facing inwards. All the time he was talking rapidly to try and hide his nervousness.

"You didn't recognise my voice on the phone, did you? I can see you're surprised it's me. I always was considered a pretty good mimic. Thought of taking it up seriously at one time—professionally, I mean. There's a lot of money in it, you know, more than in painting—especially if —"

"If you don't mind I'm in rather a hurry," Mike cut in. Chris had backed up against the desk and was drumming with his fingers on its carved edge. "Get to the point."

"I've got a friend who wants to take a trip abroad, and —"

"Go on." Chris had faltered like an actor who's forgetting his lines.

136

"This friend of mine knows where the boy is—the boy you're looking for."

"Get to the point," Mike repeated. "How much?"

Chris appeared to be put off balance at this quick transition to the actual terms of the blackmail. In fact Mike had come prepared to do a deal. He had three Banker's Drafts in his pocket for sums of respectively five hundred, a thousand and two thousand pounds.

"Well —" Chris was grasping the edge of the desk with knuckles that showed white. He ran his tongue over his lips. "My friend's figure is—six thousand pounds."

The last phrase had come out in a rush. Mike studied Chris's face impassively, nodding slowly.

"Six thousand pounds." Mike's face and voice were expressionless.

"Yes."

Mike put his head on one side as if considering the proposition.

"And what proof have I got that your friend is telling the truth?"

"The kite —" Chris ventured.

Mike shook his head. "Before I part with six thousand pounds I want a great deal more proof than that."

"All right, then." A faint note of triumph had come into Chris's voice. The interview was beginning to follow the pattern he had foreseen. "What about this?"

He took the envelope from his pocket, extracted a photograph and held it up for Mike to see. It was a postcard-size head and shoulders shot of the boy he had seen on the common. Mike stared at it for a few seconds. There could be no doubt about it. The tooth-plate, the spectacles, the wistful eyes—they were all there. Perhaps this snapshot made him look a little younger but that was the only difference. Chris was smiling as he returned the photograph to its envelope. Even the trembling had subsided. Ruby had been right. Mike had not much choice except to pay up.

"Well? What shall I say to my friend?"

Mike did not answer at once. He was listening carefully, trying to gauge whether Chris had some accomplice hiding at the back of the shop. He surely could not have been so guileless as to place himself in this position. But, apart from the grandfather clock's limping beat, the place was utterly silent.

"You can tell him this," Mike said bluntly. "If he's depending on me for his trip abroad he'd better resign himself to 'holidays at home'."

Chris's smile faded abruptly. His brief confidence had been shattered. But this time it was replaced not by nervousness but by a spark of anger.

"You'd better think again. Believe me, without my friend's help you haven't a dog's chance of finding that boy."

"Hadn't a dog's chance," Mike corrected him. He saw Chris blink and went on. "We've had nothing to go on. Now things are different."

Mike was looking at the envelope, still held in Chris's hand. Realising his intention, Chris backed round the side of the desk, so as to get it between him and Mike. As he did so he sent a pile of labels and a tray of drawing pins tumbling to the floor.

"All right. If you're not going to fork out, that's that. You can get to hell out of here."

"Not without that photograph."

Mike moved round so as to place himself between Chris and the door. Chris thrust the envelope into his breast pocket and seized the scissors from the desk.

"Don't come any nearer or I'll—I'll use them, d'you hear me? I'll use them!"

His voice was hysterical. Mike knew that his type could be as ferocious and dangerous as a wild cat when they are cornered. Keeping his eyes on the scissors he advanced on Chris round the side of the desk. Chris broke away and ran to the back of the shop, leaning against the lateral bookcase.

"Look, why don't you pay up? You can afford it. Four thousand. What do you say to that?"

Mike shook his head, then turned away as if washing his hands of the whole affair. Suddenly he snatched a large book from one of the shelves and holding it up as a shield, rushed at Chris. The artist dodged aside and nipped round the end of the bookshelf into 'the cloister'. Mike went after him. Chris was at bay now. He could not be outflanked but he had left himself with no line of retreat.

"What the hell do you want this photo for? You still won't be able to find him."

"Then why not hand it over?"

Chris shook his head obstinately. Mike charged. He saw the hand bearing the twin prongs of the scissors come slicing down towards his neck. He parried the blow with the book. The scissors glanced aside and he felt sudden fire at his right wrist. The next instant he had gripped Chris's arm with his right hand. With the other he was reaching for the young man's throat. He twisted the arm with all his strength and the scissors clattered to the floor. But with a twist like a cat Chris broke free of Mike's grip. He jumped past the step ladder on which he had been standing earlier and as Mike came lurching after him he shoved it with all his strength. This time Mike could not parry. The heavy ladder crashed down on him, its solid mahogany top step striking him on the temple. He slumped face downwards on the floor with the ladder on top of him.

Chris stared in horror at what he had done. Mike's body was

lying in a horribly unnatural position. Blood was oozing from the wound at his wrist and matting the hair on his head.

"God!" Chris breathed. "I've killed him!"

To get clear he had to clamber over the steps and past the body. Mike was utterly motionless. There was not even any sign of breathing. Chris turned, still staring downwards, and backed away till he bumped against shelves. Then he turned and ran blindly towards the door. There came the sound of the bolt being drawn and the ping of the bell. When that died away the grandfather clock took over the silence in Dubinsky's bookshop.

Chapter Nine

Dubinsky was one of those people who have to go back home on the first day of their holidays to see if they've remembered to turn the gas off, who walk out of shops without collecting their change and sometimes without even taking the parcel they've bought, who climb five flights of stairs and then have to go down to the bottom again to recollect what they went up to look for. This time he had got to the doors of the hospital before he remembered that he had forgotten the very special book he was going to take to the invalid.

When he reached his shop he blinked with surprise at the 'Closed' notice hanging inside the glass-topped door. He tried the handle. The door was not locked. His first thought as he entered was that his shop had been burgled. He'd always read that burglars leave a place in a terrible mess. Then he saw the man sitting in the chair behind his desk. Little rivulets of blood streaked one side of his face. He was trying to tie a handkerchief tightly round a badly bleeding wrist. His face was frighteningly pale.

Dubinsky pronounced a resonant Polish oath. The man looked up.

"Here. Help me tie this tight. I've got to stop this bleeding."

"Mike Hilton! What are you doing here?" Dubinsky was

still rooted to the spot with amazement. "What's happened? Has there been an accident? Where's Chris?"

"Give me a hand and then I'll tell you. We've got to phone the police quick."

At the mention of the police Dubinsky moved into action. While he bound up Mike's wrist and fetched a basin of water to wash the blood from his face Mike gave him a brief account of the incident.

"But I can't believe it," Dubinsky took his spectacles off and tried to polish them. When he had finished they were even mistier than before. "Chris wouldn't do a thing like that."

"You didn't put him up to it?"

"Certainly not!"

"What was he doing alone in the shop, then?"

"He's short of cash. I give him small jobs to do to help him out. He never sells any of his pictures. How are you feeling now?"

Mike dabbed at the spot on his head where the ladder had hit him. It was throbbing painfully and extremely tender to the touch. His head however had stopped swimming. He did not know how long he had been unconscious but it couldn't have been more than a few minutes. The time was only just after ten to one.

"Not too bad," he said. "Can I use your phone? I must telephone the police. We've lost too much time already."

"Why do you want to telephone the police?"

"To report this attack, of course. And tell them that Chris has a photo of the boy."

"You think they'll believe you?"

"They've got to."

"It's your word against Chris's. Are you—er—on very good terms with the police—"

142

Mike glared up at Dubinsky. He was picturing in his mind O'Day's sceptical expression when he heard Mike's account of this whole improbable incident.

"Can you think of a better idea?" he asked dryly.

Dubinsky leant a podgy hip on the side of the desk. "Maybe I can. I've known Chris for a long time. There's no real harm in the boy. I'd hate to see him get into trouble."

"What do you suggest?"

"The photograph is what you want, isn't it?"

"Yes, but I'm not prepared to be blackmailed for it. Not to the tune of six thousand pounds at any rate."

"Then let me talk to Chris. If I can persuade him to hand it over will you drop the idea of reporting him to the police?"

Mike bit on his lip. He pushed his injured hand inside his coat so that it was supported on the button. In that position the painful throbbing was lessened.

"After all, my friend, I think you owe me a favour." Dubinsky nodded at the books lying scattered on the floor where Chris and Mike had struggled. "Some of those books are very valuable. Do you not agree?"

"All right." Mike nodded and the ghost of a smile came on his face. "I'm sorry about your books, but don't worry, I'll pay you whatever they're worth."

"No, no, that's not important." Dubinsky put a hand up as if refusing actual cash. "Just let me have a word with Chris first—if that does not work, then you go to the police."

Mike pushed the chair back and gingerly experimented with standing on his feet. The room rocked briefly and then steadied down.

"All right. We'll try it your way."

. . . . . .

143

Following Dubinsky's directions Mike drove up into the less reputable part of Fulham and turned into a street of dilapidated houses.

"Number twenty-seven." He touched Mike's arm and pointed to a terraced house with steps to the front door and a flight going down to the basement flat. Mike pulled into the kerb and Dubinsky struggled to get the car door open.

"Shan't be a tick," he said.

"I'm coming with you."

Dubinsky twisted round to argue the point but changed his mind when he saw the expression on Mike's face. Together they walked the few yards along the pavement and Dubinsky led the way down the steps to the basement flat. The white paint of the door was peeling. Dubinsky knocked and put his ear to the wood. Then he moved to a barred window and peered into the dim interior.

"Chris! Chris! Are you there?"

"The door's always open," a voice called from above. Mike glanced up and saw a slatternly woman leaning against the front door with a baby in her arms and a cigarette between her lips.

"Oh—er—thank you." Dubinsky went to the door and tried the latch. The door opened with a creak.

Mike followed him into a gloomy room, furnished with an old settee, a bare table and some kitchen chairs. There was no carpet on the floor. A greasy gas cooker stood in one corner with dirty pots and pans on it. An easel had been placed under the window, catching what light there was. Canvasses and oblongs of hardboard littered the room. There were tubes of paint everywhere.

Dubinsky had gone to the door of a small adjoining room, where Mike could see one end of an unmade bed with grubby sheets.

144

"Chris! You there, Chris?"

Mike had walked round the easel and was looking at the almost completed portrait. It was a study of a nude woman with full breasts and generous buttocks. The face was a remarkably good likeness of Ruby Stevenson but somehow it did not seem to match the youthfully voluptuous figure beneath.

While he was looking at it Dubinsky came up behind him.

"Ruby in the nude!" he breathed. "The little devil. How did he persuade her to pose like that?"

A shadow had passed the window. The door to the flat opened to admit a hard-faced woman with an apron across her front.

"Oh, 'ullo. It's only you, then. Myrtle said there was a visitor."

"Mrs Poole." Dubinsky hurried towards her ingratiatingly. "I'm looking for Chris. Has he been back here since he left this morning?"

"This morning!" Mrs Poole's chuckle sounded like a man's —a man with bad catarrh. "'E left 'ere Monday."

"Monday. That's three days ago."

Mrs Poole nodded.

"Well where is he now? Where's he staying?"

Mrs Poole shrugged. Her eyes strayed to the portrait on the easel and she sniffed.

"Has he gone to Miss Stevenson's place?"

"Don't ask me."

"Where is she living now—do you know?"

"Well, I know she did move out of Coster Street into somewhere posh. Chris said something about Stratford Mansions. I don't know why the 'ell 'e follows 'er around like 'e does. She's old enough to be 'is grandmother."

145

"Stratford Mansions!" Dubinsky had jerked his head at Mike and was already making for the door. "Thank you, Mrs Poole."

Stratford Mansions was a newish five-storey block of flats in a roadway which had become a cul-de-sac when the Cromwell Road extension had been built. It was one step up from the council house type of building and sported a lift as well as the concrete stairway which wound up beside it. The only occupant of the courtyard into which Mike and Dubinsky hurried was a small girl playing handball against one of the walls. She missed her stroke as they went past and Mike caught her ball to stop it rolling out into the street. He walked up to her and handed it back. She took it but instead of saying a word she sent her thanks through her eyes. That satisfied Mike. It always used to madden him when Ruth had insisted, "Say thank you, Jill." What more eloquent thanks can you expect than the look of pleasure on a child's face?

Something about this kind man had attracted the little girl's attention. She turned to watch him, grasping her ball tightly, as he went to the stairway. Dubinsky had pushed his spectacles back and was peering at the list of names printed against the flat numbers.

"No Stevenson here."

"No, but there's a blank against number ninety-three. All the others have names. That must be the one."

"Fifth floor," Dubinsky grumbled. "It would be."

He pressed a squat finger on the button and they heard the lift come chuntering down.

Number ninety-three was almost opposite the lift doors. A small white card had been drawing-pinned to the outside. It read 'Miss R. Stevenson'. From inside came the steady but faint beat of a radio tuned to a jazz programme.

Dubinsky pressed the bell-push for a second. Chimes sounded within the flat. Almost at once the music ceased. But there came no sound of footsteps. After a couple of minutes Dubinsky put his hand up to ring again but Mike stopped him. Using sign language he indicated the still open lift doors, motioning Dubinsky to take it down. Dubinsky nodded and gave a wink to show that he had understood. He tramped heavily to the lift, closed the doors with great fussing and banging and sent the lift moaning downwards.

Mike pressed himself into a recess in the wall close to the door of Ruby's flat and waited. After perhaps thirty seconds he heard the Yale latch turning. There sounded a faint crack as paint parted from paint. Whoever was in the flat had not been able to resist the temptation to look out and confirm that the caller had departed. Mike lunged out of his hiding place, and got his shoulder to the door just as it was closing. In the nick of time he managed to wedge the toe of his shoe in the narrow opening.

For a moment he was pitting his strength against the person on the other side. The upper hinge protested under the strain but held firm. Suddenly the surface Mike was heaving against was whipped away from him. Thrust forward by his own effort he charged into the hall sprawling onto his hands. At the same moment a dimly seen figure slid past him out of the flat. By the time Mike had picked himself up he was already scampering down the stairs.

Cursing himself for becoming the victim of such an old trick Mike went after him, taking the stairs three at a time. Always the other man was out of sight round the next corner. Just when he thought he had him in his sights he found his way blocked by an old lady and had to steady himself to avoid bowling her over.

As he careered down the last flight of all he heard a yell and a curse ahead of him, then the sound of a heavily falling body. Racing out into the courtyard he stopped short.

The tableau ahead of him was haloed by the afternoon sun. On the ground sprawled the figure of a man. Dubinsky was just kneeling down with avuncular solicitude beside it. Near by the little girl was holding the back of her hand to her mouth, gazing in horror at what she had done. As Mike approached she turned fear-filled eyes up at him expecting a reprimand. The ball was still spinning gently at the foot of the stairway.

"Oh, God," Chris moaned, sitting up and gripping his ankle. "I've broken my ankle. That ruddy ball —"

Then Mike understood. He gave the little girl a reassuring smile, tousled her blonde hair and groped in his pocket for a half-crown.

"That's to buy a new ball," he told her. "Just in case the other one's spoilt."

"You still haven't told me the boy's name," Mike persisted.

"I tell you I don't know it."

"I don't believe you."

"All right, you don't believe me."

"Chris, don't be stupid," Dubinsky urged. "We're only trying to help you."

It was Dubinsky's afternoon for administering first aid to the injured. Between them he and Mike had hauled a wincing and protesting Chris into the lift and up to Ruby's flat. Chris had flopped on the sofa while Dubinsky brought a basin of warm water to bathe the swelling ankle. While he fetched aspirins and water Mike kept a wary eye on the young man and looked around the flat.

Ruby was doing all right for herself. The furniture in the

148

flat was good solid Victorian or Edwardian and the rugs on the floor could have been Persian. She had spent her money wisely. The freshly papered walls were covered with photographs of Variety artists, most of them adorned with affectionate inscriptions and flamboyant signatures.

Chris's attitude was one of sullen defiance. He was clearly scared of Mike and well aware that there was a score to be settled. Towards Dubinsky he showed the resentment of a petty crook who's been 'shopped' by a friend. Into the bargain he had lost his principal weapon. While manhandling him upstairs Mike had managed to get the envelope containing the photograph out of his pocket.

He had waited until Louis had administered a couple of aspirins before starting on the questions.

"Oh, sure," Chris was sneering. "You're very anxious to help me, aren't you, Louis?"

"If he isn't, why do you think he took the trouble to bring me here?" Mike snapped, at the end of his patience. "But believe me, *I* am not so concerned about you. I don't care two hoots what happens to you. All I want —"

"Is to save your own skin," Chris cut in. "I know."

At this Mike's temper broke. He seized Chris by the lapels of his jacket and hauled him to his feet so that his face was a bare six inches from his own.

"You listen to me! You're going to tell me all I —"

Chris's face contorted in agony. Under his weight the basin had tipped over and given his injured ankle a fresh twist. He put his head back and yelled. Mike felt a restraining arm on his elbow. Suddenly sickened by the whole thing he released Chris and let him fall back on the sofa.

This sordid situation was such an anti-climax after the melodramatic developments of last night and this morning. He did not believe now that Chris had any connection with the murder. The smoothly operating professional who had set him up as suspect number one for Selby's killing would never have had a hand in such an amateur attempt at extortion as this. These people were on the fringe of the big crime and thought they could see some way of cashing in on the fragmentary knowledge they possessed. The one solid fact was that somehow or other they had got hold of a photograph of the boy. Even if he did not learn any more he could take this to the police and it could be used to expedite the search.

"Of course he's trying to save his skin," Dubinsky was reasoning with Chris. "We're not all as stupid as you are. Don't you see, if you don't tell Mike all you know he'll hand you over to the police."

Chris stopped his moaning. Still rubbing his ankle he frowned up at Mike. Prompted by the pain of his ankle he seemed at last to see reason.

"Well—what is it you want to know?"

Mike held up the photograph. "Who is this boy?"

"I've told you I don't know. Ruby calls him 'Biff' but that's just a nickname. I don't know who he is." Chris switched from Mike's sceptical face to Louis. "That's the truth, Louis. I swear it."

"All right, Chris boy. Louis believes you. Now tell us what happened between you and Ruby."

"It was last Sunday night; she asked me to call round here and see her. When I got here she was all het up with excitement —"

Chris stared with vacant eyes at the far end of the room as if materialising the ghost of Ruby in his mind. Dubinsky prompted him gently. "Go on."

"She started to talk about Selby—about the murder. She said she had a pretty good idea who did it and if we played

150

our cards carefully there could be a heap of money in it for us."

Mike stared at him incredulously. Suddenly he was much nearer the heart of the matter than he had ever dared to hope.

"Did she give you any idea who it was?"

"No. But I've been thinking about this and I'm almost sure it's the man she works for. He's a sort of agent for her, you know—helps her to find customers."

"You mean he runs a call-girl racket and she's on his books," Dubinsky said resentfully.

"Ruby Stevenson a call-girl?" Mike said with a chuckle. "Don't make me laugh."

"What the hell do you know about it?" Chris spat at him fiercely. "You think the only women men want are kids with flat behinds and no bosoms who don't even know what sex is about? There's a lot more to Ruby than people think. She's got a heart for one thing and her figure—well, many a young woman would be proud of it."

"All right, Chris," Dubinsky patted him on the arm soothingly. "Did she tell you anything else?"

"She showed me the kite and the photograph."

"Did she say where she got them from?"

"No. But it must have been some relation of the boy or a member of the same family, mustn't it? And if the bloke she works for —"

"Wait a moment," Mike interrupted excitedly. "I think I'm beginning to get it. This boy—let's call him Biff—told me that he had to meet his father. Now suppose his father was the person who committed the murder then naturally Biff would have to be kept under lock and key. If he had been found it would have corroborated my story. Now if Chris thinks that the murderer was Ruby's boss —"

Mike stopped his pacing and stood over Chris again.

"Have you any idea where this man lives?"

Chris shook his head. "She's always been very cagey about him. All I know is she makes trips into the country to visit her 'sister'."

"Where? What part of the country?"

"I don't know. I was never really interested. She takes a Green Line coach, that's all I know."

"Is she with her sister now, Chris?"

"I don't know where she is, Louis. She told me to come back here after I'd seen Hilton and wait till she turned up."

Somewhere in the flat a telephone had started ringing. Chris sat up.

"That's probably her now. I think she said she might ring."

"Where's the telephone?" Dubinsky asked.

"She had it moved into her bedroom. She likes to phone from in bed. Spends hours gabbling away."

"All right," Mike said. "You'd better answer it."

"That's all very well, but what the hell do I say?"

Mike pondered for a few seconds. "Tell her you've seen me and I've agreed to pay the money. Say you'll wait for her here. Then ring off immediately."

Chris looked from Mike to Dubinsky. The old sullen expression was back on his face. Louis gave him a little nod of encouragement and a pat.

"Go on, Chris. Better do as he says."

He helped Chris to his feet, and supported him while he hobbled towards the door behind which the telephone was steadily ringing. Chris turned the handle. The shrilling of the bell was suddenly very loud. Inside the room the curtains had not been drawn and it was still dark. Chris put out a groping hand and switched on the light.

Mike had decided to keep a close watch on Chris and was close behind him. He saw the young man peer round the edge of the door. For a moment he seemed to be turned to stone, then he twisted round and, leaning against the door jamb, vomited on the floor.

"Chris!" Dubinsky called out. "What's the matter?"

Half knowing what he was going to find Mike squeezed past the retching Chris and entered the bedroom. It was the second time in a week that he had found the body of a murdered woman. But this was different. There had been a sort of clinical precision about the killing of Selby. Mike had become convinced that the disorder in the houseboat had been created after the murder. But in Ruby's room there was every sign of a passionately brutal killing preceded by a desperate struggle for life and survival. The rugs on the floor had been rucked up, pictures on the walls were broken or hanging at drunken angles. The dressing table had been overturned depositing its clutter of scents, powders, lotions and make-up on the floor. The overpowering smell of cheap toilet water drowned any other odour. The contents of the chest of drawers had been tipped out onto the floor, every dress had been ripped out of the wardrobe.

The bed was a shambles. What lay among the bloodstained pillows and bedding seemed not so much the remnant of a human being as a splash of colour added by some macabre artist to complete the apocalyptic scene. Ruby had obviously been thrown on the bed by her killer after he had done his work, and the final indignity of her attitude seemed even more atrocious than the fact of her death.

Fighting the nausea that was making his own stomach heave, Mike moved to the phone. Miraculously it had survived the struggle and still sat on the shelf by the bed. Averting his eyes from the bed he picked up the instrument.

153

"Hello."

Once again, after a brief pause, the ringing tone started up again in his ear. Without waiting he dialled 999.

"Which service do you want?"

Mike said, "Police."

Chapter Ten

Within seconds of dialling the emergency number Mike was talking to the station officer in charge of the division of the Metropolitan Police in which Stratford Mansions was situated. In point of fact the quiet voice which answered him belonged to a sergeant who was doing an inspector's job.

"Just a minute, sir. May I have your name and the address you are speaking from?"

Checked by the matter-of-fact tone (how could anyone receive the news of a murder so equably?) Mike controlled his own emotions and gave the required information. There followed a short pause while the station officer picked up a phone and arranged for the nearest police car to proceed to the address given.

"Now, sir, would you give me that information again?"

Mike repeated his brief statement. As soon as he had the gist of the situation the officer cut in on him —

"Right, sir. A patrol car is on its way to you. If you'd just be ready to admit the officers when they come. You and the other persons just remain where you are. Leave everything exactly as it is."

"Yes," Mike assured him. "I know all about that."

He put the receiver back and immediately picked it up again. He dialled the number of 'Tall Trees'.

Meanwhile the station officer had reported the matter to the superintendent in charge of the Division who in his turn had telephoned Department C.I. at Scotland Yard. By a fortunate chance Superintendent O'Day was in the office at that time, and on learning that the reported murder had occurred at an address which the local C.I.D. knew as the operating base of a call-girl he decided to undertake the investigation himself. Within five minutes, accompanied by a detective sergeant from the same department, he was being conveyed by an 'Incident Squad' car to Stratford Mansions.

A practised and systematic mobilisation of experts was being put into operation by radio and telephone. While Mike, Chris and Dubinsky sat white-faced in Ruby's 'lounge' the police surgeon, the pathologist, the photography team, the forensic experts were dropping whatever work they were doing and carefully noting down the address where a bludgeoned body awaited their analytical consideration.

Once again Mike was privileged to watch the police procedure for dealing with a murder moving into action. It was much the same as in the Thames Valley Division but now that he was in the Metropolitan Area there were slight variations. Here the whole process was speedier, more practised, a lot more impersonal.

He had barely put down the telephone after telling Ruth where he was and what had happened when there came a sharp rap on the flat door. Dubinsky trotted out to open it.

It had been 1.43 p.m. when Mike had dialled 999. The two uniformed constables from patrol car RS5 knocked on the door at 1.49. After a rapid inspection of the situation—the senior man remained in Ruby's room only long enough to confirm that she was past human aid—they confined the three witnesses to the sitting room. The younger man went out again to act as guide to the various officers who would soon be arriving.

At 1.53 the police surgeon knocked on the door. He took a quick look at the victim and then stood about with carefully assumed patience till, at a minute after two, the photography team arrived. Not till the scene of the murder had been photographed from all angles did he start his examination.

At 2.10 the pathologist, a professor from the local Medical School, hurried in and joined the police surgeon.

At 2.12 a whole bunch of experts arrived in a body—fingerprint men, a forensic scientist, various police officers specialised in the various techniques of investigation.

It was just coming up to 2.15 when O'Day made his entry, like an operatic hero stepping onto the stage soon after the curtain has gone up on the first act of a Grand Opera.

He paused inside the door to hear the report of the reserve inspector who had taken charge up till then. His eyes moved alertly over the three civilians sitting almost forgotten in the 'lounge'. Just a faint flicker of surprise crossed his face when he recognised Mike Hilton.

The flat was now as full of purposeful activity as a television set on which the weekly serial is being filmed. Inside the bedroom, a polythene sheet had been spread out and when the body had been moved onto it the photographers went to work again. The pathologist and the forensic scientists were examining the body and the bedroom for contact traces— hairs, footprints, blood or skin tissue in the fingernails. Half a dozen other officers were quietly going about their tasks, fingerprinting, ferreting, using their eyes and their noses, even helping to lift dead weights.

In the street below three patrol cars, four anonymous saloons and an ambulance were drawn up. A crowd of curious onlookers had assembled and many of them were craning their necks upwards to the fifth floor. The fire engine which had tried to get in on the act had been turned away. Some excitable citizen had misinterpreted the signs and reported a fire. The first of the crime reporters was already on the scene. He had shown his 'Yard Pass' to the man on duty down below and was now waiting outside the door of the flat.

O'Day nodded curtly to the reserve inspector to show that he'd heard all he needed to know and walked with his ponderous gait into the sitting room.

"Afternoon, Mr Hilton. So it was you who made the 999 call?"

"Yes." Mike stood up to get on level terms with the superintendent. In both their minds was the knowledge that this was the second time that Mike had been first on the scene of a murder. "I came up here with Mr Dubinsky and Mr Benson here. We were trying —"

"I'll hear your statement presently, sir," O'Day interrupted. He nodded at Mike's bandaged wrist and then at the plaster on his head. "Been in the wars again, I see, Mr Hilton."

He had turned his back before Mike even had a chance to explain the cause of his injuries. The police surgeon was waiting for him at the door of the bedroom. He had done all that was required of him—the forensic pathologist would continue examination of the body at the mortuary—and was anxious to get back to his consulting room.

". . . within one or two hours," Mike heard him murmur. "Body temperature has fallen two degrees. Severe bruising and abrasions of the head and body, possible fracture of the skull. Actual cause of death was strangulation —"

"Much discoloration?" O'Day interposed.

"No. It wasn't asphyxia. Shock due to pressure on the carotid arteries. As you know, there is no congestion in such cases."

"You'll let me have the usual report."

"Yes, yes, of course." Glancing at his watch the police

surgeon hurried out of the flat. Like a late guest arriving at a cocktail party O'Day walked, nodding to his acquaintances, into the murder room. The door closed firmly behind him.

The little French clock on the mantelpiece ticked away forty more minutes before O'Day emerged. He sat down in a comfortable chair facing the three men, found a magazine to form a flat platform on his knee and brought out his notebook and pencil.

"Now, Mr Hilton. Since you made the emergency call perhaps we'd better have your statement first."

Mike turned to Chris. "I'm sorry, Chris. I'll have to tell him about the kite and the photograph."

Chris turned away from him. His mouth was trembling and he was biting hard at his lower lip. The once brave moustache was drooping pitiably.

O'Day listened without comment to Mike's account of the finding of the kite, the phone call and the incident at Dubinsky's bookshop.

"I see," he said when Mike finished. "And this photograph. Where is it now?"

"I have it. I managed to extract it from Chris's pocket while we were hauling him up here."

"Chris. You mean Benson, I presume?"

"Yes. I call him Chris because that's what Dubinsky calls him."

"May I see it, please?"

Mike reached in his pocket and took out the photograph. He handed it to O'Day who studied it for a moment and then put it under his notebook.

"Now, Mr Benson. Will you tell me how this photograph and the kite came into your possession?"

Chris launched into a rambling and emotional account of how Ruby had shown him the kite and the photograph and promised him that they could be used to extort money from Mike. He swore that he knew nothing more about them.

"May I see your hands, please, sir?"

Mystified, Chris stretched his hands towards O'Day. The superintendent studied them carefully. They were still stained with paint and none too clean.

"And the other side, please. Thank you, that will do." He turned to Dubinsky. "Now, sir, may I have your full name and address?"

Dubinsky was so anxious to supply information that O'Day had to keep bringing him back to the point. In fact he was unable to add anything to what Mike and Chris had already said.

"Now, Mr Benson, I want you to think carefully before you answer this question." O'Day had swung round in his chair to face Chris. "How long were you alone in the flat before Mr Hilton and Mr Dubinsky knocked?"

"Not more than twenty minutes," Chris murmured almost inaudibly.

O'Day glanced up in annoyance as a uniformed constable entered from the front door.

"Excuse me, sir. A Mrs Hilton is here. She is asking to see her husband."

"Mrs Hilton?" O'Day's eyes switched suspiciously to Mike. "Did you arrange to meet her here?"

"I phoned her after I made the 999 call. She was worried about me already. I knew from experience that I was likely to be here for some time. I just wanted to put her mind at rest."

"Tell her she may have to wait a bit," O'Day said to the officer. "Let her sit in one of the patrol cars and don't allow the Press to get at her. Make sure she's properly looked after."

"Very good, sir."

"You say she called him Biff," O'Day continued, addressing himself to Chris. "Are you certain that was the name?"

"That was what she called him but it was just a nickname. For all I know it wasn't used by anyone else."

"Did she speak of the boy often?"

"No. I never heard her use the name till she showed me the photo. That was last Sunday."

"When she spoke of him was her tone—er—affectionate?"

"Not particularly."

"But you had the impression that she knew the boy herself?"

"Yes, I did."

Mike was staring past O'Day at the new arrival who had been admitted by the officer on duty at the door. He was virtually certain that it was the man who had been drinking in 'The Four Poster' on the day when he had seen Ruby Stevenson and Chris there together. With a quick look at Mike he walked straight up to O'Day.

"Ah, Bellamy," said the superintendent. "There you are at last. We've been waiting for you. Just take a look at the body, will you? I think she may be a member of your—ah—flock. I expect the pathologist is about ready to have her transferred to the mortuary."

"Sorry I couldn't make it sooner, sir. I was right out in Camden Town."

Bellamy, following the direction of O'Day's nod, moved towards the murder room. A few minutes earlier Mike had seen two officers carry in the 'shell' or provisional coffin in which the corpse would be conveyed to the mortuary. When the door was opened he could not resist a quick peep inside. On the floor lay an anonymous form neatly parcelled in a white

161

plastic sheet. Chris had seen it too and a sob escaped from his throat as the door swung to again.

"Superintendent," Mike said. "Would you regard it as improper if I made a suggestion?"

"No, Mr Hilton. What is your suggestion?" The superintendent's face expressed polite but indifferent interest.

"We were discussing this before we realised that Ruby was lying dead in the next room," Mike sat forward eagerly, his brow furrowed with concentration. "It seems almost certain that Selby Brooks's murderer was the father of this boy. When he learnt that I and the boy had met it was imperative for him to make his son disappear. Now, if he realised that Ruby had somehow got possession of a photo of Biff he must have come here to recover it. She came in and surprised him while he was searching and he killed her."

"Very interesting theory, Mr Hilton."

"But you don't agree with it?"

"If his object was to find the photograph, why was the search confined to the bedroom? If your theory holds we would expect to find the same disorder in the whole flat."

"You think there was some other motive?"

"It could have been plain murderous rage or revenge. There is every sign that the murderer completely lost control of himself in his urge to kill."

"Do you think it is the same man as killed Selby Brooks and that other girl—what was her name?"

"Della Morris. Yes, I'm reasonably confident that this is the handiwork of our friend 'Mr King'."

Mike indicated the photograph of the boy which lay under the notebook on O'Day's knee. "Well, you have a good chance of locating him now. All you have to do is publish that photo. Even if he's been shut away someone's bound to recognise him."

"There is one good reason for not doing so, Mr Hilton."

"Oh? And what's that?"

"We have to think of the safety of the boy. If a murderer is concealing him in order to save his own neck he may be in some danger."

"I see," Mike said thoughtfully. He glanced round as the detective sergeant hurried out of the bedroom.

"Something interesting here, sir," the sergeant said to O'Day in a low tone. "We found it in her raincoat. It's a receipt for cash from a store in Aylesbury dated 22nd."

O'Day took it with a perfunctory nod and placed it carefully under his notebook with the photograph.

"And we found an address book in her handbag in the kitchen."

"Good," said O'Day. "I'll have that too."

He took the small leather-bound notebook and nodded dismissal to the sergeant. He ruffled through the pages and then handed the book to Mike.

"Quite a lot of names here. I'd like you to look through them carefully and tell me whether any of them were at this party you told me about."

"At the party?" Mike repeated, puzzled.

"The murderer was probably at that party too. That's where he got hold of the newspaper you did your little trick with."

O'Day looked round enquiringly at a detective sergeant who had not appeared in the flat before and who was not admitted to the flat. He had a notebook in his hand, held open at a page somewhere near the centre.

"Got anything, Baker?"

"I've established a list of all unidentified persons who were seen to leave the premises after twelve thirty, sir. As a matter of fact my best informant was a little girl I found playing ball in the courtyard. Smart little kid. Knows how to use her eyes."

O'Day took the list and ran his eye down it. His glance flickered up to Dubinsky and Chris as if he were comparing the description with the reality.

"This tall fellow with glasses seems to have been the last to leave before these gentlemen came in. I suppose she didn't see whether he left by car?"

"She thinks he did. Yes, sir."

"Didn't get the number, of course."

"No, but she said it made an exciting noise as he drove away."

O'Day turned to Chris. "You didn't happen to meet anyone of this description on the stairs or in the lift? Tall, oldish, wearing a check suit and spectacles."

Chris shook his head. "No. I didn't meet anyone."

O'Day struggled out of the armchair and onto his feet. "Well, gentlemen, I have to accompany the body to the mortuary. After that I would like you to amplify your statements, if you will. My sergeant will take you to divisional headquarters —"

"Superintendent," Mike had also risen and was at the superintendent's elbow as he reached the door of the bedroom. "There is something I want to ask you."

"Yes. What is it?" O'Day had turned, fingers already gripping the door handle.

Mike glanced at Chris and Dubinsky. "Could we talk somewhere more private?"

O'Day hesitated and then nodded towards the kitchenette. "Let's go in there."

When the door was closed behind them he faced Mike.

"Well, Mr Hilton."

"You remember at the station at Belford," Mike began awkwardly. "You told me that Selby Brooks was er — was —"

164

"I seem to remember that I told you she was a notorious character."

"Yes. I've been wondering whether you really knew —"

"I was telling you the truth, Mr Hilton," O'Day said with a little nod. "I wasn't just talking for effect, using shock tactics, if that's what you think. She was a professional blackmailer. It's my guess that's why she was murdered."

"Well, all I can say is she—she didn't blackmail me," Mike said almost aggressively.

"No?" There was no hint of cynicism in O'Day's tone. "Well, perhaps she didn't want to. Perhaps she was in love with you, Mr Hilton. All kinds of people fall in love."

"But that's not what you think?"

Beyond the door Mike could hear the sound of bumping and the tread of heavily laden feet. He guessed that the 'shell' was being moved out to the ambulance.

"No, that's not what I think. I think she was preparing the ground. She knew you were pretty well off and ultimately, in my opinion, she'd have told you she was pregnant. Then she'd have started to blackmail you. That was the usual form, Mr Hilton."

"I—I just can't believe it," Mike said, shaking his head.

"I could be wrong of course. I could be very wrong."

"You think it possible that she had found out who 'Mr King' was and was trying to blackmail him?"

"That is a possibility I have not overlooked. We know that she was paid a sum of two thousand pounds not long ago— she purchased the houseboat with it. Even the call-girls don't come by that sort of money overnight."

O'Day was obviously anxious to go. The sounds of bumping had faded away and the flat seemed to be emptying itself of the small army of policemen who had invaded it. He contemplated Mike not unkindly. One important fact was still in his mind, preventing him from completely dismissing this young man as a suspect. Further checks had confirmed that the skin tissue and blood traces found in the fingernails of Selby Brooks tallied with Mike's. It never occurred to him that a woman with a background such as that could be passionately attracted to a man she intended to blackmail.

He said: "I'd be glad if you'd look carefully through that address book, Mr Hilton. That's where you can give me most help."

"I'm rather touched by O'Day trusting me with this," Mike said, tapping the cover of Ruby Stevenson's address book. "If I found damning evidence against myself I could easily suppress it."

"I expect he had it photocopied or got someone to copy out all the entries," Ruth answered.

They were stirring their coffee after eating in a restaurant at the western end of the King's Road. It had been nearly seven by the time Mike, Dubinsky and Chris Benson had been released from the clutches of Superintendent O'Day. Mike had half expected that Chris would be detained. He had, after all, been closeted for nearly half an hour with the dead woman and was the only person who was known to have had an opportunity of committing the murder.

"At least O'Day can't suspect you of this murder," Ruth pointed out. "You can prove that you were with Dubinsky while it was happening — or lying unconscious in his shop. How's your head, by the way? Any the better for eating something?"

"Yes. The wine helped too. It's fair to say I missed out completely on lunch. Were you worried about me, Ruth?"

"Terribly. I was sure you were walking into some sort of

166

trap. I just couldn't keep away, knowing the spot you must be in."

"Really you shouldn't have come, but I'm glad you did. How did the police treat you?"

"They were quite firm about not allowing me in but otherwise terribly considerate. I had the most trouble with a horrible little reporter. But the police gave him short shrift."

"I wish I didn't feel that O'Day still has a sneaking suspicion about me." Mike added another lump of sugar to his coffee. "If we could only locate this boy all would be plain sailing. But he refuses to have the photograph published."

"The address book doesn't help us?"

Mike flicked the pages of the book, looking at the list of names.

"O'Day seems pretty positive that the murderer was at the party in 'The Four Poster'. Strange to think that it's probably someone I know by sight. Vida, Ingrid, Sel—they're all here in this book, even Della Morris. Chatsworth . . ." Mike looked up, hesitating. "Chatsworth . . . so he was one of Ruby's clients! Well, I'm damned! Let's see if Barry's here too . . ."

Mike ran his finger down the index to the F section.

"Freeman. B. I. Freeman . . . Yes, he's in all right. I thought he would be." -

Ruth stubbed out the cigarette she was smoking in the near-by ashtray. "B. I. Freeman . . ." Her voice was soft, almost a whisper. Mike looked up at her, puzzled.

Ruth said: "Mike, I think I'm onto something! Doesn't a boy often have his father's initials, in fact very often the same christian names?"

Mike nodded, but he still wasn't sure what she was getting at.

Ruth said: "If Barry Freeman has a son then his initials

167

could very easily be B.I.—B. I. Freeman, and surely 'Biff' would be a perfectly natural nickname for him!"

Mike put the address book down on the table; he made no attempt to control his excitement.

"My God, Ruth—you really are onto something! The description of the person seen leaving Stratford Mansions was of a tall man wearing a check suit and glasses. He probably seemed older than he really was to the little girl. And if the car he drove off in sounded exciting it could very easily have been the M.G. he bought from Chatsworth last week."

"What's his address?"

Mike picked up the book and held it close to the table lamp.

"That's funny. I thought he lived in London. It says Long-acre Grange, Aston Clinton."

"Where's Aston Clinton?"

"A few miles this side of Aylesbury."

"What's the matter, Mike?"

"Aylesbury! Ruby Stevenson was in Aylesbury on the day Sel was murdered." Mike was gazing at Ruth in astonishment. "This just can't be coincidence! Come on, drink up! I'm going to phone the inspector."

"You mean the superintendent."

Mike shook his head. "Not on your life! I'm going to get old Craddock onto this!"

Chapter Eleven

Travelling at a virtuous fifty miles an hour Mike kept about a hundred yards behind Craddock's black Jaguar. Darkness had fallen as they left London behind them and he was now driving on dipped headlights. Every time the two-car convoy met traffic coming in the opposite direction he could see the heads of the two policemen outlined in the frame of the rear window.

Craddock, glad of any opportunity to help Mike, had readily agreed to see him and had listened carefully and sympathetically to Mike's information. But he had flatly declined to take any steps without contacting O'Day. Ruth and Mike had to sit nursing their impatience while Craddock's switchboard operator checked the C.I. department at Scotland Yard, the Information Room at several divisional headquarters and various other numbers where O'Day might be found. He had finally run him to earth swapping pints with Bellamy at 'The Four Poster'. Mike did not know whether to be elated or disgusted at this.

Listening to one end of the conversation he could tell that O'Day was more than a little sceptical about Mike's theory and reluctant to go so far out of London while he was just getting his teeth into this new murder case. Mike was grateful for Craddock's insistence. He made it clear that he was not prepared to let this lead go cold. Strictly speaking it was outside the Metropolitan Police area but he had informed O'Day as a matter of courtesy and so on. In the end O'Day had agreed to meet them at 'The Bull', near Gerrards Cross. He had left his black Ford outside the hotel and with an inscrutable glance at the Mercedes had climbed in beside Craddock.

Now, as they approached the built-up area of Wendover, Mike moved up closer to the tail-lights of the Jaguar.

Craddock stopped outside the police station. The bulky form of O'Day emerged from the car and hurried inside.

"I expect he's going to find out exactly where this place is," Mike explained to Ruth. He stretched his arms and clasped his hands behind his neck. She groped in his pocket for the cigarete case, took one out, and lit it.

"Not much longer now, darling. I have a feeling that this is the end of the road."

"End of one road," Mike said. "Beginning of another."

He glanced round at her, almost shyly.

"You're dead tired," she said, putting the cigarette between his lips. "Try to relax, darling."

O'Day was out of the police station within a minute. As the Jaguar moved off they could see him making signs to Craddock. The inspector took a minor road leading out of Wendover and soon they were moving into an area of hilly, more wooded country. At a road junction where a sign pointed to Stainwick Craddock made flapping gestures with his right hand and stopped the car. Mike drew in beside him as he stepped out. He walked back to the Mercedes.

"It'll be best if you wait for us here, Mr Hilton. Longacre's about half a mile up this road. The superintendent won't be long."

Mike nodded. He might have answered: "That's what I was afraid of," but he held his peace. If he'd had his way a cordon of police would have been thrown round the property before anyone moved in.

The sun had set an hour earlier but an almost full moon was riding high in the clear sky. Colour had gone from the landscape but forms and shapes showed up as clearly as in a black and white film. It was remarkable that within five minutes of turning off a main road they were in such an apparently deserted corner of the countryside.

The Jaguar's right-hand trafficator winked brassily as the inspector's clutch went in with a jerk. The police car disappeared into a narrow but well-surfaced road. Mike had not switched his engine off. Now he doused his lights, engaged first gear and followed the Jaguar.

He shadowed it for half a mile till it stopped at a set of imposing but ramshackle gates. The headlights swung round till they illuminated a crudely painted sign. "Longacre Grange. Heavy vehicles please use other entrance." The Jaguar turned in at the gates. Half a minute later Mike did the same.

The avenue led at first between a couple of open fields. Once they had been farmland but now they had been turned into cemeteries, the last resting place of hundreds of abandoned cars. They lay there in desolate rows, the moonlight barely striking a glimmer from their rusting panels. Hideously twisted wrecks conjured up horrifying pictures of high-speed crashes and trapped bodies, of cars falling over precipices or sinking slowly to the bottom of harbours while their occupants clawed at the windows. At one corner the gaunt outline of a crane loomed up. Round it the wrecks were piled twenty or thirty feet high and near by a mechanical crusher squatted like some replete monster gorged with metallic fodder.

Ruth shivered. "What a depressing place! How could anyone bear to do this to the countryside?"

Mike was slowing down. Ahead of him was a double line

of Wellingtonia trees, tall graceful conifers whose regularly planted trunks formed the columns of a cathedral-like corridor leading to the house itself a hundred yards away.

He stopped the car, opened the door and slid out of the driving seat.

"You take her now. Pull in behind that hedge so O'Day and Craddock won't see you when they leave."

"Mike!" Ruth made one last appeal. "Do you have to go in alone? I don't like this place. It gives me the shivers."

"We've been over this. O'Day obviously thinks this is a wild-goose chase. He'll never find the boy by these methods, he'll only scare Freeman off."

"Please promise to be careful. I couldn't bear it if anything happened to you now."

He stopped and kissed her lightly on the cheek. "Don't worry, poppet, nothing will."

She watched him as he moved up the avenue, walking on the springy grass under the sloping branches of the sentinel-like firs.

Craddock and O'Day had approached without ceremony, parking the Jaguar slap outside the door of the 'Grange'. Carefully drawn up in a semicircle on the broad turning-circle in front of the house were a score of well-polished vehicles. They were the pride of Freeman's collection and awaited the scrutiny of the car traders with whom he did business.

The house itself was a compact stone building, whose unity had been rather spoiled when a recent owner had built a third floor under the roof, throwing out unsightly dormer windows. They were now shuttered. Rare trees still flourished in the parkland close to the house but the gardens had been allowed to go to rack and ruin and the grass or what had once been lawn was waist high.

"Pity it's been let go like this," Craddock observed as they waited for someone to answer the bell. "Sort of place I've always dreamed of owning."

"You can have it! I wouldn't like to tackle that grass on a Sunday morning."

Craddock turned and had a hand on the heavy knocker when the fanlight above the door was illuminated from inside and a step sounded in the hall. A bolt was drawn, a chain rattled and the door swung open. The two policemen's eyes quickly took in the man who stood there — tall, bespectacled, check-suited.

"Mr Freeman?" Craddock enquired.

"That's right."

"We are police officers, sir. We think you may be able to help us with some enquiries we're making."

"Police?" Freeman's face expressed concern. "Well — er — perhaps you'd better come inside."

"Thank you, sir."

The man was obviously nervous. Craddock and O'Day exchanged a quick glance as they stepped over the threshold. Freeman led them to a room at the back of the house. It was well furnished with good solid Victorian pieces, and impeccably tidy. It had a slightly musty, unlived-in feeling. Nervously Freeman seated his guests and then stood waiting, like a condemned man on whom sentence is about to be passed.

His suspicions now fully alerted O'Day decided to exploit the advantage he felt he had.

"Now sir, we are making enquiries following the murder of a Miss Ruby Stevenson. What we would like you to tell us —"

"Murder?" Freeman interrupted. "Did you say you were investigating a murder?"

"Yes, sir," O'Day confirmed ponderously. "A murder."

"Well, thank God for that!" Freeman made his relief

173

evident. "For one ghastly moment I thought — You see in my business I buy a great number of used cars and I can't always check on their history. It's a constant nightmare that someone will unload a stolen car on me and I'll be had up for receiving."

It was not often that Craddock saw O'Day thrown off balance but he could tell now that the superintendent had lost momentum.

"Very interesting, sir. But if you will allow me to proceed. Do you know anyone of the name of Ruby Stevenson?"

"Ruby Stevenson." Freeman's brows furrowed and he pursed his lips. "The name does seem to ring a bell. Should I know her?"

"That's what we're asking you, sir." O'Day unfolded the evening paper he'd been carrying. The murder was on the front page with a portrait photograph of Ruby Stevenson. He handed it to Freeman. "Is that face known to you?"

Freeman took the photo and glanced at the headlines.

"What a ghastly thing! Wasn't there another case very similar to this not long ago?"

"Do you know her?" O'Day repeated doggedly.

"No. I don't think so."

"Have you ever been to Stratford Mansions?"

"Stratford Mansions? Where are they?"

"Just off the Cromwell Road, opposite Earl's Court."

"No." Freeman shook his head. "Definitely not."

O'Day decided to fire his torpedo. "Can you explain, Mr Freeman, how your name came to be in Miss Stevenson's address book?"

"My name was in her address book?" Freeman's slightly receding chin had dropped. O'Day wished that his spectacle lenses did not so effectively hide his eyes. "There's only one explanation I can think of. Was she by any chance a call-girl?"

"Yes. She was."

"Then that explains it, I'm afraid." Once again Freeman's relief was evident. "It's only too true that I'm known to be somewhat prone to a little of that there." He tittered briefly. "These girls swap names and addresses, you know. Sometimes one of them can supply your wants better than another. I'll wager my name wasn't the only one in that book." He paused for a moment before waggishly adding: "Was it?"

O'Day stirred uncomfortably. He was remembering that Ruby Stevenson's book had contained several names well known to the public.

"I really think that we could all do with a drink," Freeman was saying. "I know I could."

He had moved to an early Victorian wash-stand with a double-hinged lid which had been converted into a cocktail cabinet.

"What'll it be—er—I'm afraid I don't even know your names."

O'Day and Craddock rose to their feet and padded across the thick carpet like fighting bulls on their pastures.

"Whisky and water for me, please, sir. O'Day's the name. Superintendent O'Day. And this is Inspector Craddock."

"I'd prefer beer, if you've got it," said Craddock.

The windows at the front of the house offered little hope. Mike skirted the side of the building, bending low to duck under the branches of shrubs which had not been pruned for years. The yard at the back of the house seemed more 'lived in'. A couple of overflowing dustbins stood outside the back door and a cardboard carton full of empty bottles had been dumped behind it. Against the wall of an outhouse was parked the M.G. in which Chatsworth had driven him up to town at the beginning of that week.

The back door was locked and the lock felt solid. But a little farther along he found the window of the below-stairs lavatory. It had not been properly fastened. He was able to lever the bar up and release the catch. The opening was just large enough for him to squeeze through.

He felt in his pocket for his torch and switched it on. The passage outside the lavatory led past the 'usual offices' to the kitchen. It was cluttered with dirty plates and cooking utensils, as if a succession of Mad Hatter's tea parties had taken place in the house and never been washed up.

He found his way to the door which led through to the residential part of the house. Fortunately the floor consisted of stone flags, so that there was no danger of a creaking board betraying his presence. The light inside the front door at the far end of the long entrance hall was still on. To his left the door of a room had been left ajar. When he moved close to it he could see a wide section of the room.

O'Day and Craddock seemed to be getting along famously with Freeman. All three of them had drinks in their hands and the conversation had become general.

"Just one other thing I want to ask you." O'Day was placing his glass on an occasional table and reaching into his breast pocket for the envelope containing the photograph of Biff. "Have you any children, Mr Freeman?"

"Just one. A boy."

"Is he living with you?"

"I have custody, yes. But he's not with me now. He left to pay his annual visit to his mother last week."

"And where is she?"

"She's set up house in Rome." Freeman made it clear that he did not relish discussion of this subject. "It suits her—ah—temperament better."

"Have you any photographs of this boy, by any chance?"

"Of Brian? No. I'm afraid not. I'm not sentimental about that sort of thing."

O'Day turned away from the mantelpiece where a loaded ashtray had escaped the vigilance of the room cleaner. He had taken the photograph of Biff from his pocket.

"Is this your boy?"

Freeman took the photograph, gave it a quick glance and then laughed.

"Poor chap. He's not much of a beauty, is he? No, Brian doesn't wear a plate and he doesn't need spectacles. In fact, though I say it myself he's rather a good-looking kid. Now can you tell me what all this is about?"

"Just routine enquiries, sir." O'Day shot Craddock a significant glance. He obviously thought it was about time for them to depart. "Thank you very much for your help, sir. Not to mention the drink."

"I'm sorry I've been such a disappointment to you," Freeman said with easy charm. "Do at least let me fill you up again."

Mike moved away from the door. The staircase led up from halfway along the hall. It creaked beneath his weight but the state of the kitchen had convinced him that no woman shared Freeman's life.

The house gave the impression that its owner had sold it complete with furnishings. The carpets, the pictures had a sort of unity and told of more gracious living in days gone by. At one end of the first landing a flight of stairs, less massively built than the main staircase, led up to the attics. At the other end was a suite of rooms which presumably was used by Freeman, for a bedside lamp glowed in one of them.

Voices were echoing in the hall as he moved swiftly to the suite of rooms where the light was burning. It consisted of a small vestibule off which opened a large bedroom, a bath-room and what had once been a dressing room. The bedroom was obviously Freeman's den. It was in a state of wild dis-order. In the window alcove stood an escritoire on which were heaped letters and bills as if they had been emptied out of a waste paper basket. Shoes and clothes lay scattered on the floor. A whisky bottle and a fifty box of cigarettes had been parked on the bedside table. Several magazines littered the floor by the bed where they had been thrown.

Mike began to tour the room methodically, hunting for a photograph—a photograph of a boy with a metal tooth-plate and steel-rimmed spectacles. He was approaching the desk when he heard the front door slam. Immediately came the sound of Freeman's footsteps, running on the stone floor of the hall.

A Kodak folder peeped from a heap of papers on the desk. Mike picked it up, quickly extracted one of the prints. It was a snapshot of three people seated on the steps at the front of Longacre. The man was Freeman, the woman was Ruby Stevenson. The boy between them had moved his face just as the photo was taken and his features were blurred.

Freeman had moved fast. His feet were already on the stairs leading up to the first floor landing. Mike realised that if he moved out into the vestibule he would be seen from the land-ing. Quickly he thrust the Kodak folder into his pocket and looked round for some place of concealment. A long built-in wardrobe filled one side of the room. The sliding door had been moved aside to leave one end open.

He crossed the room on tiptoe, slid in through the opening. He dared not close it, for fear that the noise of the roller bearings would betray him. The best he could do was draw a dressing gown in front of him and hope that his legs were shadowed.

Freeman came into the room half running. He went straight to a solidly carpentered tallboy and, using a key from his chain, unlocked the top drawer. Mike saw him take out an automatic, slide in a magazine full of bullets and slip the weapon into his pocket. That done he opened the lower drawers and began to dig out shirts, socks, underwear which he piled on the bed.

Next he would want suits and that would mean coming to the wardrobe. Freeman turned towards him and Mike's muscles tautened in readiness. But with an impatient glance at the pile on the bed Freeman seemed to change his mind. He turned and hurried out of the room.

This was Mike's last chance to escape from the blind alley in which he had trapped himself. He was almost on Freeman's heels as the owner of the house ran onto the landing. If Freeman had turned round as he doubled up the stairs that led to the attic he would have seen Mike opening the door to the former dressing room.

Mike heard the ratle of a key in a lock somewhere on the floor above and the sound of empty suitcases bumping about. He slid into the dressing room, but kept the handle twisted so that he could emerge without noise. When a minute later he heard the swish of Freeman's feet on the carpet outside he opened the door again. From the bedroom came the rumble of the roller bearings as the wardrobe door was opened wide. Under cover of that sound he emerged from the dressing room and slipped out onto the landing.

So far no evidence that Freeman was not alone in the house. The only hope now was the set of rooms at the other end of the landing. They were all open. He twisted the three handles in turn and looked into deserted rooms filled with sheeted furniture. In the last a tall spectral form, probably a dressmaker's dummy draped with a sheet, stopped his heart

179

and made him pause. While he stood there he became aware of a low rumbling noise. It increased in volume, seeming to pass directly over his head and then die away again. To his strained nerves its sounded like some inter-continental ballistic missile rumbling on its way to the obliteration of some thriving metropolis.

The hair on the back of his head stirred, like grass fanned by some midnight wind. The rumbling had begun again; another projectile was passing overhead. In the silent, almost ghostly house this impersonal vibration was uncanny.

He moved out of the suite of rooms and stared up the staircase. At the top a door hung open with a key in the lock. That was where Freeman had gone to collect the suitcase. Mike remembered now the dormer windows he had noticed in the roof. Keeping one eye on the doorway leading to Freeman's bedroom he moved carefully up the stairs.

The landing outside the door was protected by banisters. Looking over the edge he could see down to the stone-paved hall below. From the bedroom at the end of the passage came the click of suitcase catches being fastened. He went through the door and found himself facing two more doors. One, which was open, led into a dark boxroom. From beyond the other came the persistent rumbling noise he had heard from below.

He grasped the handle, turned it noiselessly and pushed. The door opened a foot, the metallic rumbling grew in volume. He was looking into a large room with a sloping roof. The far side had been fitted up as a bedroom with bed, chest of drawers, table and chairs. The nearer portion had been turned into a child's playroom. It was littered with mechanical toys, brilliantly coloured under the single unshaded bulb that hung from the ceiling. But the centrepiece was an elaborate model railway track.

Kneeling on the floor was a nine-year-old boy dressed in a

grey pullover and grey trousers. His hand was on the lever that controlled the electric circuit and he was gazing with rapt attention at the electric train which was rumbling gaily round the track. He stopped it opposite himself and as he reached behind him for another coach to add to the train Mike saw the steel-rimmed spectacles and the earnest little face of the boy with the kite, much paler now than when he had seen him on the common.

"Biff! I thought I told you to keep that door shut."

Freeman's voice sounded from the bottom of the stairs. Mike drew back quickly and passed like a shadow into the darkness of the boxroom. He heard Biff scramble to his feet and cross the room. Father and son met in the doorway.

"I didn't open it, Dad. Honest."

"Don't lie to me," Freeman said harshly. "You can't expect me to believe it opened itself."

"It must have. I promise you I never touched it."

Through the crack between door and jamb Mike could see the boy's face turned upwards, half fearful, half appealing.

"I'll let you off on this occasion. We haven't time to argue. Get your pyjamas and washing things packed. We're moving out."

"Oh, good!" Biff's face lit up. "I'm sick of being cooped up in here. Where are we going?"

"Don't ask questions. Just do as I tell you."

Biff darted across the room, his nimble feet avoiding the toys scattered on the floor. Freeman followed him in, stepping gingerly over the model railway line. Biff dragged a case out from under the bed and started throwing pyjamas, brushes and comb into it.

"Can I take a few toys as well?"

"You can if you're quick about it. We may be away a pretty long time."

"I shouldn't bank on that," Mike said from the doorway.

Freeman whipped round. The boy stood frozen. Then he shouted excitedly to his father. "It's him, Dad! The man I told you about. He helped me get my kite down."

Biff was staring at Mike with shining, excited eyes. Freeman's expression was less welcoming.

"Take the case and wait for me downstairs, Biff. I'll deal with this gentleman."

Biff snapped the case shut. He seemed to sense the tension in the atmosphere. His eyes switched from one face to the other before he scuttled across the room and out onto the landing. Mike gave him a reassuring grin as he stood aside to let him pass. Then he walked into the playroom.

"You've made one hell of a mistake, my friend, coming here like this." Freeman's voice was casual, almost friendly. But his hand had moved to the pocket where the automatic bulged.

"I don't think so," Mike parried. "I knew that as soon as the police had gone you'd try and make a run for it."

"Clever reasoning, but you're not invited to join the party."

The automatic was in Freeman's hand now. To judge by the assured way in which he grasped it he was confident of his ability to use it. Mike saw his finger tense on the trigger. Dropping his eyes he noted that Freeman was standing just inside the oval of the electric railway circuit.

"If you want to stay alive, Hilton, move over to that bed. Lie down and put your hands behind your back. I could kill you but I'd prefer to leave you where you can be found in a couple of days."

Mike had no intention of placing himself in a position where he could be shot without trouble through the back of the skull.

"You're not going to do either," he said, playing for time. "You seem to have forgotten that it's you who's made the big mistake. Even if you did shoot me you'd never get out of the house. The police have this place surrounded."

"Come off it. You can't bluff me. If they'd had any real evidence they'd have taken me with them—or at least come with a search warrant."

There was just enough doubt in Freeman's eyes for him to check over in his mind whether he had perhaps committed some small mistake. Mike measured the distance between his own toes and the curve of the railway line.

He spoke urgently. "Della Morris was stabbed on August 12th. Your name was found in her address book. Selby Brooks was strangled on August 22nd. Your name was in her book too. Early this afternoon Ruby Stevenson was battered to death. Your name was —"

He never finished that sentence. From out on the landing where Biff, unnoticed by the two men, had been standing listening, there came a gasp and an agonised cry of disbelief and protest.

Just for an instant Freeman's attention was distracted by the boy's sobbing exclamation. Mike seized what he knew must be his only chance. He bent forward swiftly, grabbed the metal railway line and tugged with all his strength. As he dragged it towards him it struck against the back of Freeman's ankles. He tottered, fighting for his balance. He got one shot off but it passed over the head of the now prone Mike and thudded into the wall behind him. Stepping forward he accidentally put his foot on an open goods wagon, skated wildly and crashed to the ground. The revolver flew out of his hand, skidded across the wooden floor and finished up just inside the door.

Framed now in the opening Biff stared down with horror at the gun beside his feet. Freeman had already recovered himself and was lunging towards it. Mike's flying tackle caught him before he was halfway there. The two men thudded against the wainscot, a mass of lashing fists and feet. The pain from his injured wrist shot up Mike's arm like a flame. Involuntarily he winced and slackened his hold. Freeman rolled over on top of him, attempting to pin him to the floor and get fingers to his throat. Mike thrust a foot into his stomach, straightened his leg and with a heave sent him sprawling across the room. He scrambled up and tried to reach the door in time to slam and lock it in Freeman's face. He was not quick enough. The other man's weight crashed against him. Locked together the two figures reeled across the landing.

His eyes wide, Biff had shrunk back against the wall. The automatic, impelled by a flailing foot, had slithered to the base of the banisters that edged the landing.

Freeman's height and weight were telling against Mike. His glasses had disappeared somewhere during the struggle but he appeared to be able to see perfectly well without them. Mike's injured wrist was a handicap and when Freeman got a hold on it he could not help crying out with the pain. Suddenly the bigger man got a leg behind Mike and sent him crashing to the ground with thirteen stone on top of him. Mike's skull seemed to burst open and all the breath was knocked out of him.

Straddling him triumphantly Freeman looked up at Biff. "Hand me that gun!"

Biff stood and stared at a face which was familiar but which he now felt he had never seen before. The mask which Barry Freeman presented daily to the world had melted and his features were twisted in the rictus of the compulsive killer. The eyes, burning and inhuman, were like those of a hound moving in for the kill. Hypnotised, Biff went to the edge of the landing and with mechanical obedience picked up the automatic. He stood, looking at the two men. An expression of agonised uncertainty convulsed his small face.

"Come on ! Give it to me. Or, by God —"

With a sudden gesture of revulsion Biff turned and dropped the gun over the banisters. Then he twisted round and bolted down the stairs. From below came the clatter of metal bouncing off wood and then striking the stone paving of the hall.

Cursing, Freeman seized Mike's hair and began to bang his head viciously against the floor.

Waiting behind the hedge at the far end of the avenue of Wellingtonias Ruth had seen the police car leave 'Longacre Grange' and turn up the road towards Wendover. Craddock was driving fast and the sound of the engine soon died away in the distance.

When the silence returned it seemed more intense than before. The Wellingtonias could almost be heard discussing this alien presence in their midst, using their own language of long sighs, faint groans and occasional creaks. She wished the car graveyard was not so close. The horribly twisted shapes appeared to writhe in the shadows. Once there came a sharp noise as if a cracked gong had been struck. Probably, she assured herself, it was only a panel contracting after the day's heat.

She switched on the map-reading light and peeped at her watch. Only seventeen minutes since Mike had left her.

The sound of the shot was brutally clear and unmistakable. Just one shot. Somehow a fusillade would have been less sinister, less final than this single detonation followed by utter silence. Since she knew Mike had no gun it stood to reason that it had been fired by an adversary. And since it had not been followed by another it seemed equally clear that the bullet had found its mark.

Ruth became certain that Mike had been killed, that he now lay dead in the house at the farther end of the avenue. If that had happened she was not specially interested in surviving herself.

A strange mixture, Ruth was. Outwardly placid, almost to the extent of being thought dull by some people, she had a core of obstinacy which made her an implacable adversary. It had taken her to the station on the day she had walked out on Mike. Now it moved her hand to the self-starter of the Mercedes. She was shaking slightly but it was not with fear.

She reversed the Mercedes out onto the avenue, pointed its nose towards the house. Clearly through the tunnel of the trees she could see the front of the house. An arc light which illuminated the turning-circle had been switched on. She saw the door burst open and a figure come running down the steps.

It was not Mike.

She heard the sound of a self-starter and the roar as an engine burst into life. Headlights were switched on. Their beams raked the front of the house, swinging round towards the avenue.

She slipped into first gear, accelerated forward. All she could think was that Mike's murderer was getting away.

The oncoming headlights were levelled straight at her now. She moved the gear lever into second, snapped on her own headlights and accelerated hard.

Kids in California played this game for kicks, she had read once. It was a kind of Russian Roulette. You found a deserted stretch of road, started a mile apart and accelerated at full speed towards each other. It was a test of nerves. The first to steer away was 'chicken'.

As the two cars leapt towards each other at a combined

186

speed which quickly built up to eighty miles per hour Freeman's hand was on the horn button. He reckoned to blast anybody out of his way. Ruth saw the headlights bearing down on her like the eyes of a monstrous and predatory cat. She was sobbing but her foot was still hard down on the accelerator. First Jill and now Mike. In a world without them she didn't want —

At the last second she closed her eyes waiting for the crash, the annihilation, the solution . . .

The crash came, but it was beside her, outside the Mercedes, somewhere to her right. She opened her eyes. Ahead, the avenue was empty. She had to brake hard to stop the car before it crashed into the steps outside the house.

Shaking almost uncontrollably now she somehow managed to extricate herself from behind the driving seat. A curious orange light was flickering over the front of 'Longacre Grange'. It was reflected from the windows like a radiant sunset. When she turned round she saw the cause.

Halfway along the avenue one of the Wellingtonias had become a plume of fire. The bonfire at its base sent thick bubbles of boiling fire up through the branches which burst into crackling, roaring flame. She twisted away, shielding her eyes from the sight. Her sense of balance, of time and space seemed to have deserted her. She swayed and would have fallen had not firm arms gripped her.

"Oh, Ruth, Ruth!" said Mike's voice. "Thank God!"

"Oh, we knew he was our man all right," O'Day said. "I could tell that as soon as I spotted the stubs in the ashtray on his mantelpiece. They were the same brand as Ruby Stevenson smoked. Lipstick on them too."

"Then why the hell didn't you arrest him? You'd have saved me a lot of trouble."

The flames of the conflagration had died down. Members of the Aylesbury fire brigade, clad in asbestos suits, were waiting to move in on the wreckage to see whether enough was left of Barry Freeman to warrant loading him into the ambulance. O'Day and Craddock had come back from Wendover with reinforcements within a few minutes of the crash.

"Hadn't enough proof, sir." O'Day was sitting in the front of the police car, talking over his shoulder to Ruth and Mike, who were sitting in the back sipping brandy from Craddock's flask. "But then I'd hardly expect you to be familiar with the Judge's Rules. As things turned out it was you who saved us the trouble—you and madame here."

Mike gave Ruth's arm a squeeze. Her trembling had gradually subsided but she had hardly spoken a word. The only thing she insisted on was that she remain very close to Mike.

"If you'll not be needing us any more," Mike said, "I think my wife would like to get away from here."

"I think we can say this case is closed now, sir. Perhaps I'll want a statement from you, but we can think about that later."

Mike had a hand on the door ready to open it when Craddock touched O'Day's arm and pointed.

"Who's that?"

A slim shadow was flitting up the avenue towards them, its form outlined by the still flaming branches of the burning Wellingtonia. It stopped, leaning against a tree and stared hard towards the fire. The orange gleam of flame was reflected from the twin lenses of a pair of spectacles.

"It's Biff," Mike muttered. "God forgive me, I'd forgotten all about him."

"Oh, the poor little scrap!" Ruth was already half out of

the car. She started to run towards the lone figure. Shame-facedly Mike climbed out after her and began to follow.

The two police officers sat in the front seats of the Jaguar watching.

"I suppose Freeman was the father all right. But who was his mother?"

"Perhaps we'll never find that out," Craddock answered. "But, to judge by that packet of photographs Hilton found, Ruby Stevenson is the most likely candidate."

"Strange upbringing for a kid," O'Day ruminated. "I wonder what'll become of him now."

"Let's wait and see," Craddock said. "Would you like to have a small bet with me, Tiny?"

Ruth had reached the boy. She squatted down so that her eyes were level with his. His face and body were stiff with shock and incomprehension. They saw her take out a hand-kerchief and start to wipe the stains off his cheeks. He stood passively, suffering her motherly attentions. When Mike walked up the boy glanced round and stared at his face for a long time. The three of them appeared to be talking, dis-cussing something important to all of them. Then the boy took Ruth's hand. They began to walk slowly towards the Mercedes.

O'Day and Craddock turned their heads as they passed but neither officer spoke a word. They were content to be com-pletely forgotten. They watched Mike open the door on the driver's side. Biff had opened the door for Ruth. He had started to tilt the seat forward so that he could climb into the back when a gesture from Ruth stopped him. He stood back while she slipped into her seat and then, when she held her arms out to him, clambered eagerly up onto her knee. The door slammed, the starter motor whirred and the Mercedes moved slowly forward.

The two watching men saw Ruth move the boy round and press his head against her shoulder so that he would not see the smoking wreck as they passed down the colonnade of Wellingtonias.

Craddock turned to O'Day. He was smiling. "I think that's five bob you owe me, Tiny."